"It's as simple as that?" he clarified.

"One night at my place and you'll give Joanna a million quid for her charity?"

Could he put up with a pain in the butt prima donna for one night for a million quid?

"As simple as that."

Blake regarded her. His practical side was screaming at him to take the cash but the other side of him, the one attuned to doom in all its forms was wary as hell.

"You know there are thousands of men out there who would give anything to have me for a sleep over?"

She shot him a coy look from under her fringe and Blake glanced at her mouth. It had kicked up at one side as her voice had gone all light and teasy.

He didn't want that mouth *slumming* it at his place.

But one million quid was hard to turn down.

"Fine," he sighed. "But I leave in the morning for my holiday and you have to be gone."

"Absolutely," she grinned. "I promise you won't even know I'm there."

Blake grunted as his doom-o-meter hit a new high. *He sincerely doubted that.*

Dear Reader

I've always had a secret hankering to do a bodyguard story. I just adore the trope. And, whilst this book isn't a typical bodyguard scenario, I hope you like my take on it—because I've had Ava and Blake in my head in various incantations for a long time now, and it was great to finally get them down on paper.

I had a lot of fun taking mega-rich, mega-spoiled supermodel Ava and shoving her on a tiny canal boat in the UK with the only man on the planet who seems immune to her charms. I had even more fun needling private, serious, returned soldier Blake with the temptation of a woman who has absolutely no problem with baring acres of skin or leaving her lingerie all over his floating home.

I'm pleased I let Ava and Blake marinate, though. Had I written their story years ago, I don't think they'd have had the emotional complexity they do today. Because underneath Ava's hard, demanding surface is a woman who can't trust. And beneath Blake's tough, pragmatic shell is a man whose physical limitations cripple him emotionally.

Which only makes their HEA even more rewarding!

I hope you enjoy their journey to love. Oh, and London at Christmas!

Love

Amy xx

THE MOST
EXPENSIVE NIGHT
OF HER LIFE

BY
AMY ANDREWS

First published in Great Britain 2013
by Mills & Boon, an imprint of Harlequin (UK) Limited.
Harlequin (UK) Limited, Eton House, 18-24 Paradise Road,
Richmond, Surrey TW9 1SR

© Amy Andrews 2013

ISBN: 978 0 263 23598 2

Amy Andrews has always loved writing, and still can't quite believe that she gets to do it for a living. Creating wonderful heroines and gorgeous heroes and telling their stories is an amazing way to pass the day. Sometimes they don't always act as she'd like them to—but then neither do her kids, so she's kind of used to it. Amy lives in the very beautiful Samford Valley, with her husband and aforementioned children, along with six brown chooks and two black dogs.

She loves to hear from her readers. Drop her a line at www.amyandrews.com.au

Other MODERN TEMPTED™ titles by Amy Andrews:

GIRL LEAST LIKELY TO MARRY

This and other titles by Amy Andrews are available in eBook format— check out www.millsandboon.co.uk

To the Kohli family, our lovely UK friends—
Amanda, Nick, Lauren and Matthew.
Even though we live on opposite sides of the world,
your friendship warms our hearts.

CHAPTER ONE

A ROADSIDE EXPLOSION in the darkest depths of a war zone three years ago had left Blake Walker with a finely honed sense of doom. Today that doom stormed towards him on a pair of legs that wouldn't quit and a ball-breaking attitude that was guaranteed to ruin his last day on the job.

Ava Kelly might be one of the world's most beautiful women but she redefined the term *diva*.

Doing this job for her had been a freaking nightmare.

'Blake!'

Her classy Oxford accent grated and Blake took a deep breath. He went to the happy place the army shrink had insisted he find—which at the moment was anywhere but here.

Last day, man, keep yourself together.

'Ava,' he greeted as she stopped on the opposite side of the beautiful maple-wood island bench in the kitchen where he was poring over some paperwork. He'd polished the top to glass-like perfection with his own two hands. 'Problem?'

'You could say that,' she said, folding her arms and glaring at him.

Blake did not drop his gaze and admire how the arm-crossing emphasised the tanned perfection of her cleavage. Even if it was on open display in her loosely tied gossamer gown that reeked of a designer label and through which her itty-bitty, red bikini could also be clearly seen.

He did not think about how wet she was underneath it.

About the water droplets that dripped off the ends of her slicked-back hair or trekked down the elegant line of her throat to cling precariously to her prominent collarbones before heading further south.

Blake did not look.

Blake was in a good place in his life. He was fit and healthy after a long period of being neither. He was financially secure. He had direction and purpose.

He could get laid any night of the week with just one phone call placed to any of half a dozen women. He didn't need to ogle the one in front of him.

She was trouble and he'd already had too much of that.

Instead he thought about the month-long holiday he started tomorrow—no braving a clutch of paparazzi every morning, no twelve-hour days and, most importantly, no divas.

'Something I can help with?' he asked.

'Yes,' she said, raising her chin to peer down her nose at him in that way he'd got used to the last few months. 'You can ask your salivating apprentice—' she jerked her thumb in the direction of the male in question '—to put his eyes back in his head and keep his mind on the job. My friends aren't here to be gawked at. They come into the privacy of *my* home to get away from objectification.'

Blake glanced over at the three women frolicking in the fully glassed indoor pool that ran alongside the magnificent internal open-air courtyard. They were all tall, tanned and gorgeous and if they were friends of Ava's then they were no doubt models too. Between them there were only twelve triangles of fabric keeping them from being totally naked.

He glanced at Dougy, who was installing some sophisticated strip lighting down the outside of the glass and steel staircase that led from the courtyard to a mezzanine level for sunbathing. Ava was right: he was barely keeping his tongue inside his head. Not that Blake could really blame him. This had to be every young apprentice's wet dream. And he was like a kid in a candy shop.

Sunlight flooded the courtyard through the open glass roof above reflecting off the stark white décor, dazzling his eyes. For a moment Blake tuned out Ava's disapproval and admired what they'd achieved—outside a semi-detached, early-nineteenth-century terraced house, inside a vibrant contemporary home full of light and flair.

'Well?' Ava's huffy demand yanked him back to the conversation.

'Dougy,' Blake said, in no mood to humour her as her gown slipped off her right shoulder exposing more of her to his view. He kept his gaze firmly fixed on the smattering of freckles across the bridge of her perfect little snub nose placed perfectly in the middle of her delicate kitten-like face.

'His name's Dougy.'

'Well, do you think you could rein *Dougy* in? He's acting like some horny teenager.'

Blake sighed. Why was it he liked project management again? He made a note to tell Charlie no more divas. Their business was going gangbusters—they could afford to be choosey.

'Ava,' he said patiently, 'he's nineteen. He *is* a horny teenager.'

'Well, he can be that on his own time,' she snapped. 'When he's on my time, I expect him to have his head down and do the job I'm paying him for. And so should you.'

Blake contemplated telling Ava Kelly to quit her bitching and let him worry about his employees. Dougy was a good apprentice—keen and a hard worker—and Blake wasn't about to make an issue out of what was, to him, a non-issue. But he figured no one had ever used the B word around Ms Kelly—*not to her face anyway*—and he wasn't going to be the first.

Hell, what she needed was a damn good spanking. But he wasn't about to do that either.

The job was over at the end of the day, they were just putting the finishing touches to the reno, and he could suck up her diva-ness for a few more hours.

Blake unclenched his jaw. 'I'll talk to him,' he said through stiff lips.

Ava looked down her nose at him again and sniffed. 'See that you do.'

Then she spun on her heel and marched away. He watched as the edges of her gown flowed behind her like tails, her lovely ankles exposed with every footfall. Higher up his gaze snagged on the enticing sway of one teeny-tiny red triangle.

The end of the day couldn't come soon enough.

A couple of hours later Blake answered the phone to his brother. Blake rarely answered the phone while at a job site but he always picked up for Charlie. His brother might have been younger but he'd been the driving force behind their design business and behind dragging Blake out of the maudlin pit of despair he'd almost totally disappeared into a few years back.

Blake owed Charlie big time.

'What's up?' he asked.

'Joanna rang. She's really upset. One of their biggest supporters is pulling out due to financial issues and she's freaking out they won't be able to continue to run their programmes.'

Joanna was their sister. She'd been widowed three years ago when her husband, Colin, a lieutenant in the British army and a close friend of Blake's, was killed in the same explosion that had injured him. They'd been in the same unit and he'd been Col's captain. And he'd promised his sister he'd look out for her husband.

That he'd bring him home alive.

Not a promise he'd been able to keep as it turned out.

She and three other army wives had started a charity soon after, which supported the wives, girlfriends and families of British servicemen. They'd done very well in almost two years but fighting for any charity backing in the global financial situation was hard—losing the support of a major contributor was a real blow.

And losing Col had been blow enough.

Blake understood that it was through the charity that Joanna kept him alive. It kept her going. It was her crutch.

And Blake understood crutches better than anyone.

'I guess we're in a position with the business now to become patrons ourselves,' Blake said.

'Blake!'

The muscles in Blake's neck tensed at the imperious voice. He took a deep breath as he turned around, his brother still speaking in his ear.

'We can't afford the one million quid that's been yanked from their coffers,' Charlie said.

Ava went to open her mouth but Blake was so shocked by the amount he held his finger up to indicate that she wait without realising what he was doing. 'Joanna needs a *million* pounds?'

He watched Ava absently as Charlie rattled off the intricacies. By the look on her face and the miffed little armfold, she wasn't accustomed to being told to wait. But *holy cow*—one million pounds?

'I need you to move your car,' Ava said, tapping her fingers on her arm, obviously waiting as long as she was going to despite Charlie still yakking in his ear. 'I'm expecting a photographer from a magazine and your beat-up piece of junk spoils the ambience a little.'

Blake blinked at Ava's request. She'd never seemed more frivolous or more diva-ish to him and he was exceptionally pleased this was the last time he'd ever have to see her.

Yes, she was sexy, and in a parallel universe where she

wasn't an elite supermodel and he *wasn't* a glorified construction worker he might have even gone there—given it a shot.

But skin-deep beauty left him cold.

He quirked a you-have-to-be-kidding-me eyebrow but didn't say a word to her as he spoke to Charlie. 'I've got to go and shift my *piece of junk car*.' He kept his gaze fixed to her face. 'We'll think of something for Joanna. I'll call you when I've finished tonight.'

'Who's Joanna?' Ava asked as Charlie hit the end button.

Blake stiffened. He didn't want to tell Little-Miss-I've-got-a-photographer-coming Ava anything about his private life. But *mind your own business* probably wasn't the best response either. 'Our sister,' he said, his lips tight.

'Is she okay?'

Blake recoiled in surprise. Not just that she'd enquired about somebody else's welfare but at the genuine note of concern in her voice. 'She's fine,' he said. 'The charity she runs has hit a bit of a snag, that's all. She'll bounce back.'

And he went and shifted his car so he wouldn't besmirch her Hampstead Village ambience, the paparazzi blinding him with their flashes for the thousandth time.

It was close to nine that night when Blake—and *the diva*—were satisfied that the job was finally complete. The evening was still and warm. Tangerine fingers of daylight could be seen streaking the sky through the open glass panels over the courtyard. Blake was heartened that the long-range weather forecast for September was largely for more of the same.

Perfect boating weather.

Dougy and the other two workers had gone home; the photographer had departed, as had the paparazzi. It was just him and Ava signing off on the reno. Dotting all the i's and crossing all the t's.

They were, once again, at the kitchen island bench—

him on one side, her on the other. Ava was sipping a glass of white wine while something delicious cooked on the state-of-the-art cooktop behind him. She'd offered him a beer but he'd declined. She'd offered to feed him but he'd declined that also.

No way was he spending a second longer with Ava than he absolutely had to.

Although the aromas of garlic and basil swirling around him were making him very aware of his empty stomach and his even more empty fridge.

He was also very aware of her. She'd pulled on some raggedy-arsed shorts and a thin, short-sleeved, zip-up hoodie thing over her bikini. The zip was low enough to catch a glimpse of cleavage and a hint of red material as she leaned slightly forward when she asked a question. But that wasn't what was making him aware of her.

God knew she'd swanned around the house in varying states of undress for the last three months.

No. It was the way she was caressing the bench-top that drew his eye. As he walked her through the paperwork the palm of her hand absently stroked back and forth along the glassy maple-wood. He'd learned she was a tactile person and, despite his animosity towards her, he liked that.

She'd handed the décor decisions over to a high-priced consultant who had gone for the typical home-and-garden, money-to-burn classy minimalist. But it was the accessories that *Ava* had chosen that showed her hedonistic bent. Shaggy rugs, chunky art, the softest mohair throws in vibrant greens and reds and purples for the lounges, beaded wall hangings, a collection of art deco lamps, layers and layers of colourful gauzy fabric falling from the ceiling in her bedroom to form a dazzling canopy over her girly four-poster bed.

Even the fact that she'd chosen a wooden kitchen amidst all the glass and metal told him something about her. He'd have thought for sure she'd have chosen black marble and acres of stainless steel. But clearly, from the smell of dinner, Ava loved to cook and spent a lot of time in the kitchen.

Blake wasn't much of a cook but he loved wood. The family business, until recent times, had been a saw mill and his earliest memories revolved around the fresh earthy smell of cut timber. His grandfather, who had founded the mill fifty year prior, had taught both him and Charlie how to use a lathe from a very early age and Blake had been hooked. He'd worked in the mill weekends and every school holidays until he'd joined up.

He'd personally designed, built and installed the kitchen where they were sitting and something grabbed at his gut to see her hand caressing his creation as she might caress a lover.

'So,' he said as their business concluded, and he got his head back in the game, 'if you're happy that everything has been done to your satisfaction, just sign here and here.'

Blake held out a pen and indicated the lines requiring her signature. Then held his breath. Tactile or not, Ava Kelly had also been demanding, difficult and fickle.

He wasn't counting his chickens until she'd signed on the dotted lines!

Ava glanced at the enigmatic Blake Walker through her fringe. She'd never met a man who wasn't at least a little in awe of her. Who didn't flirt a little or at least try it on.

But not Blake.

He'd been polite and unflappable even when she'd been at her most unreasonable. And she knew she'd been unreasonable on more than one occasion. *Just a little*. Just to see if he'd react like a human being for once instead of the face of the business—composed, courteous, respectful.

She'd almost got her reaction this afternoon when he'd been on the phone and she'd asked him to shift his car. The tightening of his mouth, that eyebrow raise had spoken volumes. But he'd retreated from the flash of fire she'd seen in his indigo eyes and a part of her had been supremely disappointed.

Something told her that Blake Walker would be quite magnificent all riled up.

Charlie, the more easy-going of the brothers, had said that Blake had been in the army so maybe he was used to following orders, sucking things up?

Ava reluctantly withdrew her hand from the cool smoothness of the bench-top to take the pen. She loved the seductive feel of the beautiful wood and, with Blake's deep voice washing over her and the pasta sauce bubbling away in the background, a feeling of contentment descended. It would be so nice to drop her guard for once, to surrender to the cosy domesticity.

To the intimacy.

Did he feel it too or was it just her overactive imagination after months of building little fantasies about him? Fantasies that had been getting a lot more complex as he had steadily ignored her.

Like doing him on this magnificent bench-top. A bench-top she'd watched him hone day after day. Sanding, lacquering. Sanding, lacquering. Sanding, lacquering. Layer upon layer until it shone like the finest crystal in the discreet down lights.

Watching him so obviously absorbed by the task. Loving the wood with his touch. Inhaling its earthy essence with each flare of his nostrils. Caressing it with his lingering gaze.

She could have stripped stark naked in front of him as he'd worked the wood and she doubted he would have noticed.

And for a woman used to being adored, being ignored had been challenging.

Ava dragged her mind off the bench-top and what she was doing to an unknowing Blake on top of it. 'I'm absolutely...positively...one hundred per cent...' she punctuated each affirmation with firm strokes of the pen across the indicated lines '...happy with the job. It's *totally fab.* I'm going to tell all my friends to use you guys.'

Blake blinked. That he hadn't been expecting. A polite, understated thank-you was the best he'd been hoping for. The very last thing he'd expected was effusive praise and promised recommendations to what he could only imagine would be a fairly extensive A list.

He supposed she expected him to be grateful for that but the thought of dealing with any more Ava Kellys was enough to bring him out in hives.

'Thank you,' he said non-comittally.

She smiled at him as she pushed the papers and the pen back across the bench-top. Like her concern earlier it seemed genuine, unlike the haughty *can't-touch-this* smile she was known for in the modelling world, and he lost his breath a little.

The down lights shone off her now dry caramel-blonde hair pulled into some kind of a messy knot at her nape, the fringe occasionally brushing eyelashes that cast long shadows on her cheekbones. Her eyes were cat-like in their quality, both in the yellow-green of the irises and in the way they tapered down as if they were concealing a bunch of secrets.

Yeh, Ava Kelly was a *very* attractive woman.

But he'd spent over a decade in service to his country having his balls busted by the best and he wasn't about to line up for another stint.

Blake gathered the paperwork and shoved it in his satchel, conscious of her watching him all the time. His leg ached and he couldn't wait to get off it.

He was almost free. She was almost out of his life for good.

He picked up the satchel and rounded the bench-top, his limp a little more pronounced now as stiffness through his hip hindered his movement. He pulled up in front of her when she was an arm's length away. He held out his hand and gave her one of his smiles that Joanna called barely there.

'We'll invoice you with the final payment,' he said as she took his hand and they shook.

She was as tall as him—six foot—and it was rare to be able to look a woman directly in the eye. Disconcerting too as those eyes stared back at him with something between bold sexual interest and hesitant mystique. It was intriguing. Tempting...

He withdrew his hand. *So not going there.* 'Okay. I'll be off. I'm away for a month so if you have any issues contact Charlie.'

Ava quirked an eyebrow. 'Going on a holiday?'

Blake nodded curtly. The delicate arch of her eyebrow only drew his attention back to the frankness in her eyes. She sounded surprised. Why, he had no idea. After three months of her quibbles and foibles even a saint would need some time off. 'Yes.'

Ava sighed at his monosyllabic replies. 'Look, I'm sorry,' she said, picking up her glass of wine and taking a fortifying sip. Something had passed between them just now and suddenly she knew he wasn't as immune to her as she'd thought.

'I know I haven't exactly been easy on you and I *know* I can be a pain in the butt sometimes. I can't help it. I like to be in control.' She shrugged. 'It's the business I'm in... people demand perfection from me and they get it but I demand it back.'

Ava paused for a moment. She wasn't sure why she was telling him this stuff. Why it was important he understand she wasn't some prima donna A-lister. She was twenty-seven years old—had been at the top of her game since she was fourteen—and had never cared who thought what.

Maybe it was the gorgeous wooden bench-top he'd created just for her? The perfection of it. How he'd worked at it and worked at it and worked at it until it was flawless.

Maybe a man who clearly appreciated perfection would understand?

'I learned early...very early, not to trust easily. And I'm afraid it spills over into all aspects of my life. I know people think I'm a bitch and I'm okay with that. People think twice about crossing me. But...it's not who I really am.'

Blake was taken aback by the surprise admission. Surprised at her insight. Surprised that she'd gone through life wary of everyone. Surprised at the cut-throat world she existed in—and he'd thought life in a warzone had been treacherous.

In the army, on deployment—trust was paramount. You trusted your mates, you stuck together, or you could die.

'Of course,' he said, determined not to feel sorry for this very well-off, very capable woman. She wanted to play the poor-little-rich-girl card, fine. But he wasn't buying. 'Don't worry about it. That's what you pay us for.'

Ava nodded, knowing that whatever it was that had passed between them before was going to go undiscovered. Clearly, Blake Walker was made of sterner stuff than even she'd credited him with. And she had to admire that. A man who could say no to her was a rare thing.

'Thanks. Have a good holiday.'

Blake nodded and turned to go and that was when it happened. He'd barely lifted his foot off the ground when the first gunshot registered. A volley of gunshots followed, slamming into the outside façade of Ava's house, smashing the high windows that faced the street, spraying glass everywhere. But that barely even registered with Blake. Nor did Ava's look of confusion or her panicked scream.

He was too busy moving.

He didn't think—he just reacted.

Let his training take over.

He dived for her, tackling her to the ground, landing

heavily on the unforgiving marble tiles. Her wine glass smashed, the liquid puddling around them. His bad leg landed hard against the ground sucking his breath away, his other cushioned by her body as he lay half sprawled on top of her.

'Keep your head down, keep your head down,' he yelled over the noise as he tucked her head into the protective hollow just below his shoulder, his heart beating like the rotor blades of a chopper, his eyes squeezed shut as the world seemed to explode around him.

Who in the hell had she pissed off now?

CHAPTER TWO

EVERYTHING SLOWED DOWN around her as Ava clung to Blake for dear life. Her pulse wooshed louder than Niagara Falls through her ears, the blood flowing through her veins became thick and sludgy, the breath in her lungs felt heavy and oppressive, like stubborn London fog.

And as the gunfire continued she realised she couldn't breathe.

She couldn't breathe.

Her pulse leapt as she tried to drag in air, tried to heave in much-needed oxygen. She tried to move her head from his chest, seek cleaner air, but he held her firm and panic spiralled through her system. Her nostrils flared, her hands shook where she clutched his shirt, her stomach roiled and pitched.

Then suddenly there was silence and she stopped breathing altogether, holding her breath, straining to hear. A harsh squeal of screeching tyres rent the pregnant silence, a noisy engine roared then faded.

Neither of them moved for a moment.

Blake recovered first, grabbing his leg briefly, checking it had survived the fall okay before easing off her slightly. 'Are you okay?'

She blinked up at him, dazed. 'Wha...?'

Without conscious thought Blake undertook a rapid assessment. She had a small scratch on her left cheekbone with a smudge of dried blood but that wasn't what caused his stomach to bottom out. A bloom of dark red stained her top and his pulse accelerated even further.

'Oh, God, are you hit?' he demanded, pushing himself up into a crouch. He didn't think, he just reached for her hoodie zipper and yanked it down. Just reacting, letting his training taking over. The bullets had hit the building high but they'd penetrated the windows and in this glass and steel interior they could have ricocheted anywhere.

'Did you get hit?' he asked again as her torso lay exposed to him. He didn't see her red bikini top or the body men the world over lusted after; he was too busy running his hands over her chest and her ribs and her belly, clinically assessing, searching for a wound.

Ava couldn't think properly. Her head hurt, her hand hurt, she was trembling, her heart rate was still off the scale.

'Ava!' he barked.

Ava jumped as his voice sliced with surgical precision right through her confusion. 'I think it's...my hand,' she said, holding it up as blood oozed and dripped from a deep gash in her palm, already drying in sludgy rivulets down her wrist and arm. 'I think I...cut it on the wine glass when it smashed.'

Blake allowed himself a brief moment of relief, his body flooding with euphoria as the endorphins kicked in—*she wasn't hit*. But then the rest of his training took over. He reached for her injured palm with one hand and pulled his mobile out of his back pocket with the other, quickly dialling 999.

An emergency call taker asked him which service he wanted and Blake asked for the police and an ambulance. 'Don't move,' he told her as he awkwardly got to his feet, grabbing the bench and pushing up through his good leg to lever himself into a standing position. He could feel the strain in his hip as he dragged his injured leg in line with the other and gritted his teeth at the extra exertion.

'I'll get a cloth for it.'

Ava couldn't have moved even if her life depended on it. She just kept looking at the blood as it slowly trickled out of the wound, trying to wrap her throbbing head around what had just happened. She could hear Blake's deep voice, so calm in the middle of the chaos, and wished he were holding her again.

He returned with a clean cloth that had been hanging on her oven door. He hung up the phone and she watched absently as he crouched beside her again and reached for her hand.

'Police are on their way,' he said as he wrapped the cloth around her hand, 'So's the ambulance.' He tied it roughly to apply some pressure. 'Can you sit up? If you can make it to the sink I can clean the wound before the paramedics get here.'

'Ah, yeh…I guess,' Ava said, flailing like a stranded beetle for a moment before levering herself up onto her elbows, then curling slowly up into a sitting position. Her head spun and nausea threatened again as she swayed.

'Whoa,' Blake said, reaching for her, his big hand covering most of her forearm. 'Easy there.'

Ava shut her eyes for a moment concentrating on the grounding effect of his hand, and the dizziness passed. 'I'm fine now,' she said, shaking off his hand, reaching automatically for the back of her head where a decent lump could already be felt. She prodded it gently and winced.

'Got a bit of an egg happening there?' Blake enquired. 'Sorry about that,' he apologised gruffly. 'I just kind of reacted.

Ava blinked. Blake Walker had been magnificent. 'I'm pleased you did. I didn't know what was happening for a moment or two. Was that really gunfire?'

Blake stood, using the bench and his good leg again.

'Yep,' he said grimly. A sound all too familiar to him but not one he'd thought he'd ever hear again. Certainly not in trendy Hampstead Village. He held his hand out to her. 'Here, grab hold.'

Ava didn't argue, just took the proffered help. When she was standing upright again, another wave of nausea and dizziness assailed her and she grabbed him with one hand and the bench with the other. She was grateful for his presence, absorbing his solidness and his calmness as reaction set in and the trembling intensified. His arm slid around her back and she leaned into him, inhaling the maleness of him—cut timber and a hint of spice.

She felt stupidly safe here.

'Sorry,' she murmured against his shoulder as she battled an absurd urge to cry. 'I don't usually fall apart so easily.'

Blake shut his eyes as she settled against him. Her chest against his, their hips perfectly aligned. She smelled like wine and the faint trace of coconut based sunscreen. He turned his head slightly until his lips were almost brushing her temple. 'I'm guessing this hasn't been a very usual day.'

Her low shaky laugh slid straight into his ear and his hand at the small of her back pressed her trembling body a little closer.

'You could say that,' she admitted, her voice husky.

And they stood like that for long moments, Blake instinctively knowing she needed the comfort. Knowing how such a random act of violence could unsettle even battle-hardened men.

The first distant wail of a siren invaded the bubble and he pulled back. 'The cavalry are here,' he murmured.

Blake stuck close to Ava's side, his hand at her elbow. 'Watch the glass,' he said as a stray piece crunched under his sturdy boots. Her feet were bare, her toenail polish the same red as her bikini.

He could hear the sirens almost on top of them now,

loud and urgent, obviously in the street. He flicked on the tap and removed the cloth. 'Put it under,' he instructed. 'I'll go get the door.'

An hour later Ava's house was like Grand Central Station— people coming and going, crossing paths, stepping around each other. Uniformed and plain-clothed police went about their jobs, gathering evidence. Yellow crime-scene tape had been rolled out along the wrought-iron palings of her front fence and there were enough flashing lights in her street to outdo Piccadilly Circus in December. They reflected in the glass that had sprayed out onto the street like a glitter ball at some gruesome discotheque.

And then there was the gaggle of salivating paparazzi and the regular press who'd been cordoned off further down and none too happy about it either. Shouting questions at whoever happened to walk out of the house, demanding answers, calling for an immediate statement.

Safely inside, Ava felt her head truly thumping now. They'd been over what had happened several times with several different police officers and her patience was just about out. Her agent, Reggie Pitt, was there—a pap had rung him—to *protect her interests*, but it was Blake she looked to, who she was most grateful to have by her side.

'Is there anyone you know who'd do this to you or has reason to do this to you?' Detective Sergeant Ken Biddle asked.

Blake frowned at the question. The police officer looked old as dirt and as if nothing would surprise him—like one or two sergeant majors he'd known. But Blake had felt Ava's fear, felt the frantic beat of her heart under his and didn't like the implication.

'You think there's *any* reason to shoot up somebody's house and scare the bejesus out of them?' he growled.

The police officer shot him an unimpressed look before returning his attention to Ava. 'I mean anyone with a grudge? Get any strange letters lately?'

Ava shrugged. 'No more than usual. All my fan mail goes to Reggie and he hands anything suss on to you guys.' Reggie nodded in confirmation of the process.

Blake stared at her. '*You* get hate mail?'

Ava nodded. 'Every now and then. Pissed-off wives, guys who think I've slighted them because I didn't sign their autograph at a rope line, the odd jealous colleague. Just the usual.'

'But no one in particular recently?' Ken pressed.

Reggie shook his head. 'No.'

'We'll need to see them all.'

Reggie nodded. 'You guys have got a whole file of them somewhere.'

Ken made a note. 'I'll look into it.'

'Excuse me,' a hovering paramedic interrupted. 'We'd really like to get Ms Kelly to the hospital to X-ray her head and get her hand stitched up.'

The police officer nodded, snapping his notebook shut. 'Do you have somewhere you can stay for a while? I would advise you not to return here while the investigation is being carried out and the culprits are still at large. Hopefully we can close the case quickly but until then lying low is the best thing that you can do.'

Reggie shook his head. 'Impossible. She's up for a new commercial—she has a call back in LA in two days. And she's booked on half a dozen talk shows in the US next week to promote her new perfume.'

Blake bristled at the agent's obvious disregard for his client's safety—wasn't he supposed to put Ava first? But the police veteran was already on it.

'Cancel them.'

Reggie, who was a tall, thin streak with grey frizzy hair and round wire glasses sitting on the end of his nose, gawped like a landed fish. 'You don't just cancel, Detective Sergeant' he said, scandalised.

'Look, Mr Pitt, in my *very* long experience in the London Metropolitan Police force I can tell you that the best way to avoid trouble is to not go looking for it. Your client enjoys a high public profile, which, unfortunately, makes her *very* easy to find. Every pap in London knows where she lives, for example.'

'I'll get her a private security detail,' Reggie blustered.

'That is of course your prerogative,' the policeman conceded. 'But my advice would still be to lie low, which, by the way, would also be the advice any security person worth their salt would give you.'

Blake decided he liked Ken Biddle after all. He seemed solid. He obviously knew his stuff and didn't suffer fools gladly. And he clearly thought Reggie was an A-grade fool.

Reggie shot the police officer an annoyed look before turning to Ava. 'I'll get you booked into a hotel, darling. Get some security organised first thing in the morning.'

Blake also decided Reggie was an A-grade fool. 'I don't think you're listening, *mate*,' Blake said. 'I think the detective sergeant knows what he's on about. It sounds like it might be best for her to go dark for a while.'

'Ava, darling,' Reggie appealed to her. 'I think they're making a mountain out of a molehill.'

'Someone freaking shot up her house,' Blake snapped. 'Aren't you supposed to have her best interests at heart?'

'It's in Ava's best interests to keep working,' Reggie said through gritted teeth.

Ava's head was about to explode as they discussed her life as if she weren't there. Her hand throbbed too and she felt incredibly weary all of a sudden. She just wanted to lie down somewhere dark and sleep for a week and forget that somebody had shot up her house. Her beautiful, beautiful house.

'Do you think I could just go to the hospital and get seen to first?' she interrupted them.

It was all the encouragement the paramedic needed. 'Right. Question time is over,' he said, stepping in front of them all, and Ava could have kissed him as he took over as efficiently as he'd bandaged her hand earlier. 'We're taking her to the nearest hospital.'

Reggie shook his head. 'No. Ms Kelly sees a private physician on Harley Street.'

The paramedic bristled. 'It's nine o'clock at night. Ms Kelly needs an X-ray, possibly a CT scan. She needs a hospital.'

'The nearest hospital is fine,' Ava assured the paramedic, before Reggie could say any more.

'Are you okay to walk to the ambulance?' the paramedic asked her.

Ava nodded. 'I can walk.'

Blake checked his watch. He could be home and officially on holidays within half an hour. He could almost taste the cold beer he had waiting in his fridge to celebrate the end of having to deal with Little-Ms-Red-Bikini.

Except Ava Kelly looked far from the diva he'd pegged her as right now.

She looked pale and shaken, her freckles more pronounced. The small cut on her cheekbone was a stark reminder of what had happened to her tonight and part of him felt wrong walking away. Leaving her in the clutches of her shark-like agent. He hesitated. She wasn't his responsibility; he knew that. He'd simply been in the wrong place at the wrong time and she was a big girl—what she chose to do next was none of his business.

But he didn't feel she was going to get the wisest counsel from good old Reggie.

'You need me for anything else, Detective Sergeant?' he asked.

Ken shook his head. 'I have your details here if I need to contact you.'

Blake nodded. That was that, then. Duty discharged. But before he could say goodbye her hand reached out and clutched at his forearm. 'Can you come with me?'

Blake looked at her, startled. *What the?*

Sure, he'd felt wrong about leaving her but he hadn't expected her to give him a second thought now she was surrounded by people to look out for her. And even though the same part of him—the honourable part—that had urged him to join the army all those years ago somehow felt obligated to see she was okay, the rest of him wanted nothing to do with Ava Kelly and her crazy celebrity life.

They were done and dusted. He was free.

He was on holiday, for crying out loud.

Not to mention he'd had enough of hospitals to last him a lifetime.

But her yellow-green eyes implored him and the doom he'd felt earlier today pounced. He sighed. 'Sure.'

Blake strode into the hospital half an hour later. He'd waited for the mass exodus of press chasing the blue lights of the ambulance at breakneck speed before he followed at a more sedate pace. Then he'd parked his car well away from the main entrance on one of the back streets. He wasn't sure why but when he spotted the bright lights of cameras flashing into the night as he got closer he was pleased he had.

Being photographed nearly every day on his arrival at Ava's and questioned *every freaking day* as to their relationship when clearly he was just the guy running the reno had been bad enough. He didn't need them spotting his car then adding two and two together and coming up with five.

He entered the hospital and enquired at the front desk and a security guard ushered him along the corridors to Ava. He clenched his hands by his side as he followed. Hospitals weren't exactly his favourite places and the antiseptic smell was bringing back a lot of unpleasant memories.

They stopped at a closed door where two other hospital security personnel stood, feet apart, alert, scanning the activity at both ends of the corridor. They opened the door for him and the first person he saw was Reggie speaking to a fresh-faced guy, clearly younger than his own thirty-three years, wearing a white coat and a harried expression. Reggie was insisting that a plastic surgeon be made available to suture his esteemed client's hand.

'That hand,' he said, pointing at the appendage in question, 'is worth a lot of money. I am not going to allow some *junior* doctor to butcher it any further than it already is.'

The doctor put up his hands in surrender. 'I'll page the on-call plastics team.'

'I need a *consultant*,' Reggie insisted. 'Someone who knows what they're doing.'

Blake caught a glimpse of the doctor's face as he backed out of the room. He looked as if he truly regretted coming to work today.

Blake knew exactly how he felt.

He was beginning to think Reggie was actually the bigger diva out of the two of them. He was surprised Ava put up with it. In three months he'd seen her fire an interior decorator, a PA and a personal trainer because they'd all tried to manage her. But she just lay docilely on the hospital trolley and let Reggie run the show.

He wasn't used to seeing her meek and mild.

But he supposed having your house shot at while you were inside it was probably enough to give anyone pause.

At least there was some colour in her cheeks now.

Ava looked up from her hand to discover Blake was in the room. 'Oh, hi,' she said, levering herself up into a sitting position.

The last half an hour had passed in a blur and she'd been unaccountably anxious lying in the CT scanner. The doctor had assured her it was clear but it wasn't until right now she felt as if it was going to be okay. She hadn't been able to stop thinking about the way Blake had pushed her to the ground. It played over and over in her head.

He'd just reacted. In a split second. While she'd been confused about what was happening he was diving for her, pulling her down. She was on the ground before the noise had even registered as gunfire.

'I thought you'd skipped out on me.'

He returned her smile with a fleeting one of his own. It barely made a dent in the firm line of his mouth. Ava wondered how good he would look with a real smile. Would it go all the way to his dark blue eyes? Would it light up his rather austere features? Would it flatten out the lines on his forehead where he frowned a lot? Puff up the sparseness of his cheekbones? Would it break the harsh set of his very square jaw?

'I said I'd be here.'

Ava blinked at his defensive tone, his dialogue as sparse as his features. A man of few words.

'Everything check out okay?' he asked after a moment or two.

This time he sounded gruff and he glanced at Reggie, who was talking on his mobile, as if he was uncomfortable engaging in small talk in front of an audience. Ava was so used to Reggie being around, she barely noticed him any more.

'CT scan is fine,' she said. 'Just waiting for a plastic surgeon for the hand.'

He nodded and she waited for him to say something else but he looked as if he was done. Then Reggie finished his call and started talking anyway. 'I've booked you into your usual suite,' he said. 'We'll organise for a suitcase to be brought to you tomorrow.'

Ava watched the angle of Blake's jaw tighten at the announcement. 'I thought the point of lying low was to *not* go to any of her usual places?' Blake enquired.

The hardness in his tone made Ava shiver. *And not in a bad way.* Blake Walker was a good looking man. Not in the cut, ripped, metrosexual way she was used to. More in a rugged, capable, tool-belt-wearing kind of way. The fact that Blake Walker either didn't know it or didn't care about it only added to his allure.

The fact that Mr-Rugged-And-Capable was looking out for *her* was utterly seductive.

It had been a long time since someone had made her feel as if *she* mattered more than her brand. Her mother had cut and run when she'd been seventeen, leaving her to fend for herself in a very adult world, and Ava had never felt so alone or vulnerable.

Sure, she'd coped and it had made her strong and re-silient—two things you had to be to survive in her world. But tonight, she didn't have to be any of those things because Blake was here.

'They have very strict security,' Reggie bristled. 'Ava will be perfectly safe there.'

Blake snorted in obvious disbelief. 'Have you cancelled her commitments yet?'

Reggie took his glasses off. 'I'm playing that by ear.'

'You know, in the army you learn that you don't secure an object by flaunting it in front of the enemy. I think you need to take the advice of the police and have her lie low.'

'If Ava put her career on hold for every whack job that ever wrote her a threatening letter she wouldn't have had much of a career.'

'Well, this whack job just signed his name in automatic gunfire all along the front of her house. I think her safety has to take precedence over her career for the moment.'

Ava had to agree. Frankly she'd been scared witless to-night. She took Reggie's advice on everything—he'd been with her a long time—but in this she needed to listen to the guy who had crash tackled her to the ground to keep her safe.

Who believed her safety was a priority.

Reggie hadn't been there. He couldn't understand how frightening it had been.

'I've known Ava a long time, Mr Walker,' Reggie said. 'A lot longer than you. And she's stronger than you'll ever know. She'll get through this just fine.'

'He's right, Reggie,' she said as the silence grew.

Just because she was strong, it didn't mean she was going to go down into the basement while she was home alone to investigate the thing that had gone bump in the middle of the night.

Because that was plain stupid.

And she hadn't had longevity in a career that wasn't known for it by being stupid. Strength also lay in knowing your limitations and accepting help.

After a solid sleep she might be able to think a little straighter, be a little braver, but tonight she just needed to feel safe.

'I'm pretty freaked out,' Ava continued. 'I think listening to the advice of the police is the best thing. At least for tonight anyway.'

'So where are you going to go, Ava?' Reggie demanded. 'You can't go back to your home and everyone else you know in London is as famous as you.'

Ava didn't even have to think to know the answer to that question. She just reacted—as Blake had done earlier tonight. 'I can go to Blake's.'

CHAPTER THREE

BLAKE GAPED AT Ava as her yellowy-green gaze settled on his face. *'What?* No.' He would rather amputate his other leg than have Ava Kelly as a house guest.

'Just for the night,' she said.

Blake shook his head. 'No.' She sounded so reasonable but he had to wonder if the bang to her head had sent her a little crazy.

He was on holiday, for crying out loud.

Reggie—bless him—looked at his client askance. 'Absolutely not!' he blustered. 'You don't know this man from a bar of soap.'

Blake watched as Ava pursed her perfect lips and shot her agent an impatient look. 'I have seen this man—' she pointed at Blake '—almost every day for the last three months. That's the longest relationship I've had with *any* man other than you, Reggie. This man—' she jabbed a finger in his direction again '—pulled me down to the ground and *shielded me with his body* while some nutcase fired bullets at my house.'

'And thanks to him you have a cut face, a gash in your hand that requires stitching and an egg on the back of your head the size of a grapefruit.'

Blake bit off the bitter *you're welcome* that rose to his lips. He didn't expect thanks or praise for yanking her to the ground. His military training had taken over and he'd done what had to be done. What anyone with his background would have done. But he didn't expect to be accused of trying to maim her either.

Ava reached her hand out to Reggie and he took it. 'I was frightened, Reggie. Petrified. I couldn't…*breathe* I was so scared.' She'd been like that after her mother left—terrified for days. Then she'd hired Reggie. 'He makes me feel safe. And it's just for tonight.'

Reggie looked as if he was considering it and Blake began to wonder if he was invisible. 'Er, excuse me…' he interrupted. 'I don't know if either of you are interested but I said no.'

'You were the one who said she should lie low,' Reggie said, looking at him speculatively, clearly coming around to his client's way of thinking. 'You said the point was for her not to go to any of her usual places.'

Blake could not believe what he was hearing. They were both looking at him as if it were a done deal. As if his objections didn't matter in the face of the fabulous Ms Kelly's needs.

'I meant wear a wig, don some dark sunnies, throw on some baggy clothes and book herself into some low-rent hotel somewhere under a different name.'

'Please,' Ava said, the plea in her gaze finding its way directly to the part of him that was one hundred per cent soldier. 'I feel safe with you.'

'She feels safe with you,' Reggie reiterated, also looking at Blake, his hands in his pockets.

Blake shut his eyes and shook his head. 'No.' He opened his eyes again to find them both looking at him as if he'd just refused shelter to a pregnant woman on a donkey. 'For God's sake,' he said. 'I could live in a dive for all you know.'

Ava shrugged. 'I don't care.'

Blake snorted. 'Right. A world-famous supermodel who insisted on four thousand quid apiece tap fittings is happy to slum it?'

She shrugged again, looking down her nose at him this time, her famed haughtiness returning. 'I can slum it for a night.'

Blake's gaze was drawn to her mouth and the way it clearly enunciated each word. Her lips, like the words, were just…perfect. Like two little pillows, soft and pink with a perfectly defined bow shape. But somehow even they managed to look haughty—cool and mysterious. As if they'd never been touched. Never been kissed.

Not properly, anyway.

Kissed in a way that would get that mouth all bent out of shape.

If she really wanted to slum it—he could bend her perfect mouth well and truly out of shape.

A flicker of heat fizzed in his blood but he doused it instantly. Women like Ava Kelly didn't *really* want to slum it—no matter how much they thought they might. And he wasn't here for that. He'd entered into a contract with Ava to do the renos on her home. Nothing more.

Certainly not open up *his* home—*his* sanctuary—to her. And he'd held up his end of the bargain.

Duty discharged.

'I'm on holiday,' he said, his voice firm.

But Ava did not seem deterred. She just looked at him as if she was trying to figure out his price—and he didn't like it. Not one little bit.

'One million pounds,' she said.

Blake blinked, not quite computing what she'd just said. She actually *had* been figuring out his price? 'I'm sorry?'

'I'll give you that million pounds your sister needs.'

'Ava!' Reggie spluttered.

Blake gave an incredulous half-laugh, a half-snort. *'What?'*

Ava rolled her eyes. 'It's simple. I've had a very traumatic evening and I don't feel safe. I don't like not feeling safe.' It reminded her too much of when her mother left and she was supposed to be past that now. 'But you made me feel safe. And my gut tells me that means something. I've survived a long time in a cut-throat industry by going with my gut. So what's it going to be? You want the money or not?'

'Ava,' Reggie warned.

'Relax,' Ava told him. 'It's for a charity. It's all tax deductible.'

'Oh…well, that's okay, then.'

Blake shook his head as the heat that fizzed earlier flared again, morphing into white-hot fury. 'No,' he said through gritted teeth, 'it's not okay. You think you can just buy people? Just throw some cash around and get what you want?'

She shrugged that haughty little shrug again and he wanted to shake her. 'Everyone has a price, Blake. There's nothing wrong with that. This way we both get something we want.'

Blake ran a hand through his close-cropped hair. Joanna called it dirty blond and was forever trying to get him to grow it longer now he was out of the army. But old habits died hard.

Joanna.

Who he'd already failed once.

He'd told Charlie he'd think of a way to help their sister and the charity that meant so much to her—to all of them. And it was being presented to him on a platter.

By the devil himself. In the guise of a leggy supermodel.

A very bratty supermodel.

'You don't even know what the charity is,' Blake snapped, trying to hold onto his anger as his practical side urged him to take what was on offer.

'Yes, I do,' she said. 'I looked it up after we spoke earlier. A charity that supports our soldiers and their families. Very good for my profile, right, Reggie?'

Reggie nodded. 'Perfect.'

Blake had been in enough war zones to know when he was fighting a losing battle. He also knew he should do the honourable thing and offer her safe haven for free. But he resented how she'd manipulated him and if she could drop a cool mil without even raising a sweat then, clearly, she was good for it.

Still…it all sounded too good to be true.

'It's as simple as that?' he clarified. 'One night at my place and you'll give Joanna a million quid for her charity?'

Could he put up with a pain-in-the-butt prima donna for one night for a million quid?

'As simple as that.'

Blake regarded her. His practical side was screaming at him to take the cash but the other side of him, the one attuned to doom in all its forms, was wary as hell.

'You know there are thousands of men out there who would give anything to have me for a sleepover?'

She shot him a coy look from under her fringe and Blake glanced at her mouth. It had kicked up at one side as her voice had gone all light and teasy.

He didn't want that mouth *slumming* it at his place.

But one million quid was hard to turn down.

'Fine,' he sighed. 'But I leave in the morning for my holiday and you have to be gone.'

'Absolutely.' She grinned. 'I promise you won't even know I'm there.'

Blake grunted as his doom-o-meter hit a new high. *He sincerely doubted that.*

'*This* is where you live?'

Ava stared down at Blake's apparent abode floating in the crowded canal. They'd slipped out of a private exit at the back of the hospital into a waiting taxi after her hand had been sewn up with four neat little sutures and she'd been discharged. Blake had refused to tell even Reggie where he lived and she'd been too overwrought to care but even so *this* was a surprise. If someone had told her this morning she'd be spending the night on the Regent's Canal in Little Venice she'd have laughed them out of her house.

'You wanted to slum it.'

Ava took in the dark mysterious shape. 'People *actually* live on these things?'

'They do.'

Ava realised she couldn't have picked a better place to hide away—no one she knew would *ever* think to look for her here. But still…

She *was* used to five-star luxuries and, while she could forgo four-thousand-pound taps, basic plumbing was an absolute must. 'Please tell me there's a flushing toilet and a shower with hot water?'

'Your fancy suite looking better and better?'

Ava was weary. It was past midnight. She'd been shot at, grilled by the police as if she were somehow at fault, then poked and prodded by every person wearing a white coat or a shiny buckle at the hospital.

She didn't need his taunts or his judgement.

Yes, she'd bribed him. Yes, she'd told him she could handle it. Yes, she was used to her luxuries. But, come on, she just needed to stand under a hot shower and wash away the fright and the shock of the day.

Why couldn't he be like any other salivating idiot who was tripping over himself to accommodate her? But, oh, no, her knight in shining armour had to be the only man on the planet who didn't seem to care that she was, according to one of the top celebrity magazines, one of the most beautiful women of the decade.

And she was just about done with his put-upon attitude. He was getting a million bucks and bragging rights at the pub to the story—embellished as much as he liked because she was beyond caring—of the night Ava Kelly slept over.

She felt as if she was about to crumple in a heap as the

massive dose of adrenaline left her feeling strung out. All she wanted was a little safe harbour.

So, he didn't like her. She couldn't exactly say he was her favourite person at the moment either, despite his heroics.

Life was like that sometimes.

'Look, you're angry, I appreciate that. I railroaded you. But you have the distinct advantage of having being shot at before. I'm sure you're used to it. I'm sure it's *just another day to you.* Me, on the other hand…the only shooting I'm used to is from a camera lens. I promise I'll be out of your hair in the morning, but do you think in the interim you could just lose the attitude and point me in the direction of the hot shower?'

He didn't say anything for a moment but she could see the clenching and unclenching of his jaw as a streetlight slanted across his profile. 'You never get used to being shot at,' he said.

Ava blinked. His words slipped into the night around them with surprising ease considering the tautness behind them. It was a startling admission from a man who looked as if he could catch bullets with his teeth.

It struck her for the first time that he might have been more deeply affected by the incident than she'd realised. But his jaw was locked and serious. He didn't look as if he wanted to talk about it.

She did though—she really did. Suddenly she needed to talk about it as if her life depended on it.

Debrief—wasn't that what they called it in the army?

'Were you scared?' she asked tentatively, aware of her voice going all low and husky.

She was greeted with silence and she nodded slowly when he didn't answer, feeling foolish for even thinking that a brief burst of gunfire would rattle him. Charlie had told her Blake had been to war zones. He'd no doubt faced gunfire every day.

'Sorry, dumb question…'

The silence stretched and she was just about to say something else when he said, 'No, it's not.' Ava blinked at his quiet but emphatic denial.

'Any man who tells you that gunfire doesn't scare him is lying to you.'

Ava stared for a moment. If that had been Blake's impression of scared she had to wonder what level of danger would be required to actually make him look it.

Or maybe he just wasn't capable of strong emotion? *And wasn't that a big flashing neon warning sign?*

'But…you were so…' she cast around for an appropriate word '…calm.'

He gave a short laugh. She'd have to have been deaf not to hear the bitter edge. 'I'm sure my sergeant major, who chewed my arse off every day when I was a green recruit, would be more than pleased to hear that.'

He was being flippant now but she wasn't in the mood—she was deadly serious. 'I thought I was going to die,' she whispered.

His eyes were hooded as he stared at her and she wished she could see them, to connect with him. 'But you didn't,' he said.

His reminder was surprisingly gentle—not facetious like his last remark. 'Thanks to you,' she murmured.

Their gazes held for the longest time. It was quiet canal side and she realised they were standing close—close enough to feel as if they were the only two people in the world after what they'd been through together. To feel united. She waited for him to make some throwaway comment about the house saving her butt or the gunman being a lousy shot. He looked as if he was gearing up to say something.

But he seemed to think better of it, dragging his attention back to the longboat. She watched him step into the bow of the boat, then make a production of unlocking the door before he finally looked at her.

'You want that shower or not?'

The fridge was empty bar a six-pack of beer and Blake gratefully freed one of the bottles as the dull noise of shower spray floated towards him through the distant wall. He sat heavily on the nearby leather armchair, easing his leg out in front of him as he swivelled the chair from side to side. He was not going to think about Ava Kelly naked in his shower.

He was going to drink his beer, mentally plot his course for tomorrow, then crawl into bed.

Or the *couch* as the case might be.

Not his big comfortable king-sized sleigh bed he'd crafted with his own two hands—helping him forget the sand and the heat and the pain and the memories—specially customised for the specs of the wide beam canal boat he'd restored. He could hardly make a guest—a female guest—sleep on the couch. Even if it was large and long and comfortable.

Especially considering Ava was shelling out one million pounds for the dubious *privilege*.

He could certainly hack it for one night. For one million quid he could hack just about anything.

Dear God—he was prostituting himself. A leggy blonde with killer eyes, money to burn and someone wanting her dead had made him an offer he couldn't refuse and he'd rolled over quicker than a puppy with a tummy scratch on offer.

He took a swig of his beer as he dialled his brother's number. 'It's after midnight.' Charlie yawned as he picked up after what seemed for ever. 'Someone better be dying.'

'Only me,' Blake snorted. Then he proceeded to fill his brother in on the events of the evening including the details of the company car Charlie was going to need to pick up from the backstreets near the hospital.

Charlie seemed to come awake rapidly and found Blake's predicament hilarious after ascertaining everyone was okay. 'What is it about you that makes people want to shoot you? I swear to God, only you, brother dearest, could land yourself in such a situation.'

'Oh, it gets worse,' Blake informed his brother as he filled him in on the facts that had resulted in him cohabiting with one of the world's most beautiful women.

'Okay, let me get this straight. *She's* giving *you,* giving Joanna, a million quid to sleep at *yours* for the night.'

Blake shrugged. 'Essentially.' Charlie laughed and Blake frowned, suddenly angry with the world. 'What's so bloody funny?'

'Sounds like a movie an old girlfriend dragged me to once a lo-o-ong time ago. That one with Robert Redford and Demi Moore.'

Blake rolled his eyes. 'She's not asking for sexual favours, you depraved bastard. She's *scared.* She just needs to feel safe for the night. To hide away for a bit.'

'So you're not going to end up in bed together?'

The vehement denial was on Blake's lips before he was even conscious of it. 'I wouldn't sleep with her if we were the only two people left on earth.'

Blake could feel his brother's eyebrow rise without having to see it. 'Why not? I would and I've been happily married for a decade.'

Blake knew his brother would no sooner sleep with Ava Kelly than he would. He was as besotted with Trudy now as he had been ten years ago. 'Sure you would.'

'Okay,' his brother conceded. 'Hypothetically. You gotta admit, she looks pretty fine in a bikini.'

'She's a snooty, heinous prima donna who caused us endless trouble with all her first-world crap,' Blake said, lowering his voice. 'I don't care how good she looks in a bikini.'

'Maybe you should.' Suddenly Charlie's voice was dead serious. 'It's okay to let yourself go every now and then, Blake. Being beautiful and rich and opinionated isn't a crime. That's our demographic, don't forget.'

Blake shifted uncomfortably in his seat. He'd seen so much poverty and desperation in his ten years serving his country. It felt as if he was selling out to admit his attraction to a woman who represented everything frivolous and shiny in a society that didn't have a clue how the other half lived. But he was too tired to get into all of that now.

'She's here for one night and, in case you've forgotten, she's a client.'

His brother snorted. 'Not any more, she's not. Which makes it perfectly okay to…take one for the team, so to speak. How long has it been since you got laid?'

Blake shook his head, not even willing to go there. Just because he chose *not* to spend every night with a willing woman didn't mean he was about to die from massive sperm build-up as his brother predicted. He worked hard every day and came home every night to a place that he'd created that was far removed from the hell he'd known in foreign countries.

That meant something these days. More than some cheap sexual thrill.

Besides, Ava Kelly was so off-limits she might as well be sitting on the moon. If he wanted to get laid, he could get laid. He didn't need to do it with a woman who'd bugged him almost from the first day of their acquaintance.

No matter what vibe he suspected ran between them.

'Is Trudy awake?' Blake tisked. 'You know, your raging feminist wife who I happen to like much more than you? She'd be disgusted by your attitude.'

'She thinks you need to find a woman too. One who can tie you in knots and leave you panting for more.'

Blake didn't say anything for a long time. 'She's in *trouble*, Charlie,' he said as he contemplated the neck of his beer. 'She just needs to feel safe.'

Charlie was silent for long moments too. 'Then just as well she chose one of Her Majesty's best.'

'No,' Blake said. 'I'm just a builder, remember? *And* I'm on holiday. If she didn't come with a million-dollar price-tag attached I'd have walked away.'

Charlie laughed and Blake felt his irritation crank up another notch. 'Whatever helps you get through the night with Ava *freaking* Kelly in the next room.'

Blake snorted at the undiluted smugness in his brother's voice. 'I hate you.'

'Uh-huh. Ring me in the morning before you set out. I want details.'

Blake grimaced. 'Right, that's it, I'm telling Trudy, you grubby bastard.'

Charlie laughed. 'Are you kidding? She's going to want to know every minute detail. She has a huge girl crush on Ava Kelly.'

Blake sighed, briefly envying his brother's easy, loving relationship. 'Maybe she can come here for the night and they can play house together.'

Charlie laughed. 'Only if I can watch.'

Blake shook his head. 'Goodnight.'

'Night,' Charlie said and Blake could hear the laughter in his voice. 'Don't do anything I wouldn't do.'

Blake hung up the phone, not bothering to answer. There was no risk of that. He was tired. *And* annoyed. He wanted this night over and done with. He wanted her gone.

He did not want to *do* anything with Ava Kelly.

Blake lifted the bottle to his mouth and threw his head back, drinking the last mouthfuls in one guzzle. He contemplated getting another one but the shower spray cut out, spurring him into action.

He needed to change the sheets on the bed. And he needed to be out of his bedroom before she was done.

Five minutes later he'd just pulled the coverlet up over the fresh sheets and was reaching for a pillow to change the case when he sensed Ava watching him. He glanced behind him where she leaned heavily against the doorway as if it was the only thing keeping her up.

'You don't have to give me your bed,' she said, the world's weariest smile touching the corners of her mouth. 'Really. Any horizontal surface will be fine.'

He'd loaned her an old shirt and some loose cotton boxers and his clothes had never looked so good. The shirt slipped off one shoulder, outlined her small perky breasts and fell to just below her waist. The band of his obviously too big boxers was drawn by the string to its limits then turned over a couple of times, anchoring low on her hips. A strip of flat tanned belly was bare to his gaze.

And a lot of leg.

Not chicken legs like those he sometimes caught on the telly when shots of skinny models walking up and down catwalks came on the news. They were lithe and shapely. And a perfect golden brown—like the rest of her. He'd avoided looking at them the last three months but it was kind of difficult now they were standing inside his bedroom.

And he'd always been a leg man.

Oh, the irony.

He dragged his gaze up. Her hair was damp and looked as if it had been finger-combed back off her forehead, her face was scrubbed clean, her freckles standing out, her cheeks a little pink from the hot water, the tiny nick a stark reminder of why she was here.

She could have been the girl next door except somehow, even in a scruffy T-shirt, baggy boxers and her eyelids fluttering in long sleepy blinks, she managed to look haughty.

To exude a you-can't-touch-this air.

Should have had that second beer.

'How's the head?' he asked, ignoring her protest, returning his mind and his eyes to the job at hand, stripping the case off the pillow.

'Sore,' Ava said, pushing off the door frame to the opposite side of the bed, grabbing the other pillow and stripping it, managing it quite well despite the handicap of her bandaged hand.

Blake quelled the urge to tell her to leave it. He didn't want her here in his bedroom. Not while he was in it too. It all seemed too domesticated—*too normal*—especially after being shot at only a few hours ago. The bed was big and empty. Big enough for the two of them. And the night had been bizarre enough without him wondering how many times he could roll Ava Kelly over on it.

Or how good those legs would feel wrapped around his waist.

'Did you take those tablets the doc gave you?'

She nodded. 'Just now.' Then she yawned and the shirt rode up a little more. He kept his gaze firmly trained on her face. 'Sorry. I'm so tired I can barely keep my eyes open.'

Blake knew intimately how shock and the effects of adrenaline could leave you sapped to the bone. He threw the pillow on the bed, then peeled back the covers. 'Get in. Go to sleep.' *Soon it will be morning and you'll be gone.* 'You'll feel better tomorrow.'

She smiled at him again as she threw her pillow on the bed. 'I couldn't feel any worse,' she said, crawling onto the bed, making her way to the middle on her hands and knees. Blake did not check out how his shirt fell forward revealing a view right down to her navel.

He just pulled up the covers as Ava collapsed on her side, her sore hand tucked under her cheek, eyes closing on a blissful sigh, her bow mouth finally relaxing. 'Night,' he said.

She didn't answer and for a moment he was struck by

how young she looked. For the first time she didn't look haughty and untouchable—she looked humble and exhausted.

Vulnerable.

And utterly touchable.

Who in the hell would want to kill her? Or had they just been trying to scare her? In which case it had worked brilliantly. Something stirred in his chest but he didn't stay long enough to analyse it.

Ava *freaking* Kelly was lying right smack in the middle of his bed—no way was he sticking around to fathom weird chest stirrings. Or give his traitorous body any ideas.

He stalked towards the door, an image of her long legs keeping him company.

Don't look back. Don't look back.

'Blake.'

Crap. He halted as her soft voice drifted towards him. *Don't look back. Don't look back.*

'Thank you,' she said, her voice low and drowsy.

Blake locked tight every muscle he owned to stop from turning around. He didn't need a vision of her looking at him with sleepy eyes from his bed. Instead he nodded and said, 'See you in the morning.'

Then continued on his way out of the room.

He did not look back.

CHAPTER FOUR

AVA'S PHONE WOKE her the next morning and for a moment she was utterly confused by her surroundings. What was the time? What day was it? Where the hell was she?

Where the hell was her phone, for that matter?

Her head felt fuzzy and her eyes felt as if they'd been rolled in shell grit. If this was a hangover then it was a doozy. The distant trilling of her musical ringtone didn't help. Inside her woolly head, her brain knew that it needed answering but her body didn't seem to be responding to the command to do something about it.

Then a shirtless Blake walked into the room and it all came crashing back to her. The gunshots, the police, the hospital.

Little Venice. Canal boat. Big, big bed.

His hair was damp as if he'd just had a shower, she noted absently as he strode towards her. And he had a hairy chest. Not gorilla hairy, just a fine dusting of light brown hair over meaty pecs and continuing down his middle covering a belly that wasn't ripped but was still, nonetheless, firm and solid. The kind of belly a man didn't get from the gym.

She stared at his chest as it came closer. The men in the circles she moved in were *all* ripped and smooth—every muscle defined, all hair plucked or waxed into submission. It took a lot of upkeep. Whereas Blake didn't look as if he'd ever seen the inside of a salon.

She'd bet her last penny Blake was the kind of guy who thought grooming belonged in the domain of people who owned horses.

'Yours, I believe,' he said, striding towards her and passing it over.

Ava took it with her good hand, ignoring its ringing for a moment. 'What time is it?' she asked.

'Time to go.' His voice was low and serious—brooking no argument. 'I'll make you a coffee.'

And then he turned on his heel and left her staring after him. *Obviously not a morning person.*

Ten minutes later, with Detective Sergeant Biddle's caution weighing on her mind, Ava followed her nose and her growling stomach in the direction of the wild earthy aroma of freshly ground coffee beans. With nothing as basic as a mirror in his room she'd pulled her messy bed-hair back into an equally messy ponytail and hoped Blake didn't have any wild expectations of what a supermodel should look like first thing in the morning.

She needn't have worried—he barely acknowledged her, instead enquiring how she drank her coffee, then handing her a mug. 'Thank you,' she said automatically, wrapping her bandaged hand around it even though the morning already held the hint of another warm day.

He didn't acknowledge that either so she wandered over to one of the two cosy-looking, dark-leather armchairs and sank into its glorious depths. She watched his back as he stared out of the large rectangular picture window above the sink in the kitchen area.

She could just make out the bustle of London traffic over his shoulder—could just hear it too. The sights and the sounds of the city gearing up for another work day. She soaked it in for a moment, preferring the low hum to the ever-expanding quiet inside the boat.

Her gaze fell to his broad shoulders.

She'd never really speculated about what lay beneath

his clothes before—she'd been too busy wondering why he seemed completely immune to her. *Off the market? Playing hard to get? Gay?* But there'd been something about his naked, work-honed chest this morning that was more than a little fascinating.

With his back stubbornly turned, Ava had no choice but to look around her. She sat forward as she did, inspecting the luxurious interior. It was nothing like the old cheap and cheerful clunker she'd been on as a teenager with a friend's family—wider too if her memory served her correctly.

Everything about the interior screamed class. High quality.

Money.

The three stairs down which she'd trudged last night as she'd entered the boat opened into a very large, open-plan saloon dominated by two classy leather armchairs and gorgeous wide floorboards. It was the floors that drew her eye now—a gorgeous blonde wood polished to a honey sheen. In contrast the walls were dark-grain wood panelling until halfway up, then painted an elegant shade of champagne.

A massive flat-screen television sat in a narrow , built-in smoky glass and curved chrome cabinet on the wall opposite her along with a bunch of other expensive-looking gadgetry. On the other side of it, and sitting out from the wall slightly, was an old-fashioned pot-belly stove that no doubt heated the entire boat in winter.

The saloon flowed into a galley-style kitchen, all granite and chrome with no expense spared on the high-end appliances from the full-sized fridge to the expensive Italian coffee machine. They gleamed in all their pristine glamour.

Opposite the kitchen, on her side of the boat, was a booth-style table, with red leather bench seats.

Beyond the dining and kitchen area was a smaller saloon. A dark-leather sofa, looking well worn and comfy, dominated the space. A pillow and some bedding were folded at one end, reminding Ava that Blake had given up his bed for her last night.

Another coffee table with a massive laptop and piles of paper appeared to act as a work space. At right angles to the couch, on the wall that divided off the living area from the rest of the boat, stood a chunky wooden bar. The bottom boasted ten, mostly full, rows of wine and above that was a shelf crammed full of every alcoholic spirit known to man.

Beyond the wall she knew was the bathroom, and beyond that his bedroom. What was beyond that, she didn't know. The back of the boat, she guessed. What was that called? The stern?

Ava dragged her wandering mind back to the interior. All the dark leather, chrome and granite gave it such a masculine feel, like a den or a cave, yet the use of blonde wood and large windows gave it light and space. It was hard to believe that such a small area could feel so big.

Blake had done a fantastic job.

For she had absolutely no doubt that Blake had been responsible for the gorgeous interior—it had his signature all over it. She only had to look at the nearby coffee table to know that. It had been constructed out of a thick slab of dark timber complete with knots. It reminded her of the craftsmanship of her kitchen bench and she placed her coffee mug on it, then ran the flats of her palms across the polished surface.

It was absolutely stunning. She couldn't not touch it.

She glanced up at Blake—still contemplating the London traffic. Clearly he wasn't going to make conversation.

'I'm sorry I barely noticed the boat last night. It's... gorgeous.'

Blake should have known it was too much for her to just drink her coffee and let him call her a cab. He hadn't slept very well last night, which had done nothing for his mood. He took a calming breath and turned round to face her.

She was sitting in the lounge chair cross-legged. His

shirt was still falling off one shoulder and acres of golden leg were on display.

She really needed to go.

Ignoring Ava's considerable charms when she'd been a picky, exacting client had been easy enough. Ignoring them when she was a damsel in distress and in the confines of his boat—not so easy.

'Thank you,' he said.

Ava waited for him to elaborate some more but nothing was forthcoming. 'I'm assuming it's all your own work?' she prodded.

Blake nodded. 'Yes.'

'Hobby, passion or business?'

Blake wondered if she'd shut up if he told her the truth. 'Therapy.'

Ava blinked. That she hadn't expected. She wanted to know more but, as Blake checked his watch, she doubted he was a man who elaborated. 'Is it a narrow boat? I went on one when I was thirteen. It seems wider than what I remember?'

Blake stifled a sigh. 'It's a wide beam,' he said. 'It's twelve foot across. Most narrow boats are about half that.'

'Yes…I remember there wasn't a lot of space…a wide beam seems like a much more liveable option?'

He shrugged and her eyes tracked the movement of his very nice broad shoulders. He'd tucked her head right in under them last night and they'd felt so solid around her—as if they really could stop bullets. She could still remember how safe she'd felt under their protection.

'It depends what you want. Wide beams can restrict your travel options. Not all canals are made for wider boats.'

Ava was about to ask more but Blake drained the rest of his coffee, placed the mug on the sink, then turned to her and said, 'You done?'

Ava, whose mug was almost empty, understood the implied message. *Time to go.* Her night was up. She too drained the contents of her drink, then held the mug out towards him. 'That was delicious. Do you think I could possibly have another? I'm not really a morning person. Coffee helps.'

Blake contemplated telling her no. Something he doubted Ava Kelly had ever heard. But his innate manners won out. He strode towards her and took the mug, turning away from her and her temptingly bare shoulder instantly. He set about making her another cup, conscious of her gaze on his back the entire time.

It unsettled him. *Blake didn't like being unsettled.*

'That was Ken Biddle on the phone.'

Blake, who had been trying to tune her out, turned at the news. 'They got him?' he asked hopefully.

'No.' She shook her head and the ponytail swung perkily.

Blake had a thing for ponytails.

'But they have some promising leads,' she said. 'They're confident they're closing in.'

'That's good, then,' Blake said, turning back to the coffee machine, away from ponytails.

'He thinks I'll only need to lie low for a few more days.'

A presentiment of doom settled around him at the casual note in her voice. 'What are your plans?' he asked, stirring in her three sugars.

Ava watched as Blake's shoulders straightened a little more. She took a calming breath. The second Ken had asked her to keep her head down for a little longer there'd only been one option for her. 'Well, actually...I was hoping I could...stay here.'

Blake dropped the teaspoon and it clattered against the stainless-steel sink. *No. Freaking. Way.* He turned slowly around, careful to couch his distaste at the idea in neutrality. 'But I'm going on holiday,' he said, determined to be firm but reasonable.

'Exactly,' Ava nodded. 'That's why it's perfect—don't

you see? I could boat sit for you, at least until they find the person who shot up my home anyway. I can be anonymous here—certainly no one's going to be looking for me on the Regent's Canal and it'll look like someone's still home here, for a little while anyway. It's win-win.'

'The boat *is* my holiday,' he said, trying to stay calm in the face of her barefaced cheek. 'I'm going up the Kennet and Avon to Bath, giving the boat her first decent run since I finished the fit-out.'

Ava was only temporarily discouraged as the appeal of spending some time afloat, traversing the English countryside on Blake's gorgeous boat, took hold.

If she had to lie low, she might as well do it in style, right?

'Even more perfect. I can come with you.'

This time Blake didn't even bother to act as he stared at her as if she'd lost her mind. Had she seriously just invited herself along on his holiday? 'No.'

'Oh, come on, Blake, please?' Ava climbed out of the chair, feeling at a distinct disadvantage with him glowering down at her. 'It'll just be for a few days and you won't even know I'm here, I promise.'

Blake folded his arms as she neared. He hadn't believed that statement last night and, after a horrible sleep on his couch, he believed it even less this morning. 'No.'

'Look, I'll pull my weight. Seriously, I can help with locks and things. They're much easier with an extra set of hands. And I can...I can cook,' she said, desperately hoping that the way to this man's heart—or his empathy at least—was through his stomach. 'I am an *excellent* cook.' She marched over to his fridge. 'I can keep you well fed,' she said as she opened it, 'while you—'

Ava blinked. The fridge was bare save for a mauled six-pack of beer and a carton of milk.

'Good luck with that,' he said dryly.

Ava turned to face him as the door closed. 'You have no food?'

'I'm expecting a delivery in the next hour or so. It'll stock me up for the trip.'

'Yes, but…what do you normally eat?'

Blake shrugged. 'I have coffee. And there's plenty of places to eat on the riverside.'

Ava shook her head. Oh, man, he was going to want to marry her after a few days of her cooking. 'In that case,' she tisked, 'you definitely need me along for the ride.'

Blake could not believe what he was hearing. 'So, Ava Kelly supermodel, darling of the paparazzi, is going to be content to act like some anonymous little hausfrau-cum-first-mate, cooking and cleaning and being a general dogs-body?'

Blake refused to think what other services she might be able to render.

Ava folded her arms too. 'I think I could manage it for a few days.' She wasn't going to be swayed by his taunts. She'd been called worse things and had worked incredibly hard since she was fourteen. Getting away with him for a few days was the perfect solution.

'Reggie won't like it,' Blake warned.

She gave him one of her haughty, down-the-nose looks. 'You leave Reggie to me.'

Blake rubbed a hand through his hair at her persistence. Just his luck to be saddled with a woman who wasn't used to hearing no. 'Look,' he said, changing tack. 'You want to lie low on a canal boat for a few days? I think that's a great idea. Knock yourself out. There's plenty along here for hire.'

Ava was starting to get ticked off. People didn't usually argue with her so much. They were generally falling over themselves to agree with her. But not Blake. Oh, no.

And she didn't understand why. She knew, in the way that women did, that he found her attractive. And it hadn't been in the way he checked her out, rather in the way he'd *avoided* checking her out. Which was just as telling.

And, *when she hadn't been miffed by it*, she'd admired him for it.

He'd been the consummate professional and that had been a nice change. A man talking to her as if she had a brain and an opinion that mattered and who dealt with all her little niggles and foibles with patience and efficiency was a rare find. He hadn't been condescending. He hadn't humoured her. He'd been straight up. Yes or no or I'll get back to you.

But, sheesh, would it seriously be that repugnant to spend a few days in her company?

'Yes, but *you're* on *this* boat,' she said. Ava walked slowly towards him. She had to make him understand just how last night had shaken her. 'I feel safe with you, Blake.' She pulled up in front of him, standing close enough to reach out and touch him, far enough away not to freak him out. 'If this guy…this person…does happen to find me… if he tried to harm me…or snatch me…'

Ava shuddered just thinking about it. She didn't like knowing there was someone out there who wanted to hurt her. And she was more than happy to lie low until they were caught.

'Don't get me wrong, I wouldn't go down without a fight. I'd kick and scream like a madwoman. But a little extra protection never goes astray, right?'

Blake gaped at the fairy dust she was snorting. *The woman didn't have a clue.* 'Are you crazy? I only have *one* leg. If he *snatches* you, I'm going to be next to useless. My days of running fast are long gone.'

Ava blinked at him and looked at his legs. She'd noticed him limping occasionally but had just figured he'd injured himself somehow. 'You…do?'

'You didn't *know*?' He lifted the jeans on his left leg to

reveal the titanium skeleton of his artificial limb. 'Why do you think I limp?' he demanded.

She looked at it askance, as if it were some unsightly blemish. He supposed someone who made a living out of defining physical beauty would be uncomfortable when confronted with physical imperfection. And then she looked at him with something akin to pity in her eyes and ice froze in his veins.

'Not so pretty, huh?' he taunted as he let the fabric drop back down.

Ava felt awful. She hadn't realised. Her cheeks pinked up—he must think her terribly self-involved. Not only had he pulled her to the ground last night, but he'd also given up his bed for her. Both actions completely without regard for his own safety or needs.

'How'd it happen?' she asked, searching his face.

'It doesn't matter,' he growled.

It *mattered* to her. 'Did it happen when you were deployed?'

Blake glared at her for a moment before answering. 'Yes.'

Ava didn't know what to say without sounding trite or macabre. She settled for, 'I'm sorry,' but even that sounded inadequate. 'I had no idea.'

Blake dismissed her apology with an annoyed wave of his hand. 'It's not your fault,' he said.

'That doesn't mean I can't be sorry it happened.'

Blake was taken aback by the quiet conviction in her voice. So many people said sorry as if it was the standard platitude expected of them. Ava sounded as if she really meant it. 'Thank you,' he said. 'But clearly, I'm not the type of protection you need.'

Ava frowned. 'Are you kidding? You're a war hero.'

He snorted. 'I'm not a hero.' He was so sick of the way that was bandied around. 'I was just in the wrong place at the wrong time.'

'You get blown up and live to tell the tale? That's pretty heroic if you ask me.'

'Nah. That just makes me lucky.' *Unlike his brother-in-law.*

Ava didn't believe that for a moment. She couldn't even begin to imagine the resilience it must have taken to recover from something so life-altering. 'Well, it'll do me,' she said.

Blake was just about over her stubborn insistence. Time to stop being Mr Nice Guy. 'No,' he said, turning away from her to stare out of the window above the sink. *Case closed.*

Ava was even more convinced now that Blake Walker was her man. But how did she get through to him when his resistance seemed impenetrable? She stared at the set of his shoulders casting around for something…anything.

In desperation an idea came to her and she threw it down like the last card she knew it was. 'I noticed yesterday when I was researching your sister's charity that they don't have a high-profile patron?'

His back stiffened noticeably and Ava felt a moment of triumph. Ah, *that* got his attention. *Joanna.* He'd reacted the same way yesterday when she'd asked who Joanna was.

His *sister* was the chink in Blake's armour.

Blake turned around slowly and glared at her and she was even more convinced.

'So?' he said, his voice dropping dangerously low.

She shrugged. 'Every successful charity needs a patron. A big name. Take me with you until the police give me the all-clear and I'll do it. I'll become their patron. I'll attend every event and fund-raiser, I'll represent their interests, speak on their behalf, I'll work tirelessly.'

Blake was once again left speechless by Ava's impulsive offer. Joanna would be over the moon to have a woman of Ava's stature on board. 'Let me get this straight,' he clarified. 'For a few nights on *this* boat you're going to not only give a million pounds to my sister's charity but commit to being its patron?'

Ava nodded. 'Yes.'

Blake shook his head incredulously. 'Why? If you're really concerned about your safety, it'd be much cheaper and a lot less work for you to hire a professional bodyguard.'

'I'm not afraid of hard work, particularly in the name of a good cause,' she said, stepping in a little closer to him, to try and convey how strongly she felt. 'And I can afford it. As for the professional, I don't need one. I just need to lie low. But I also need to feel safe while I'm doing it and *you,* as we've already established, make me feel safe. I can't put a price on that.'

Blake still couldn't wrap his head around it all. 'I think you have more money than brains.'

Ava smiled at him then as she sensed him weakening. 'Please, Blake. If not for me, then do it for Joanna.'

Blake shook his head at her as soft lips curved up in perfect unison, nothing haughty about them now. Clearly she thought she had him all figured out. And certainly she'd found his soft underbelly. She'd made him an offer he couldn't refuse—and she knew it.

But if she thought she could just crook her finger at him and he'd come running, then she could think again. 'Does anyone ever say no to you, Ava?'

Ava let herself smile a little bigger. Was that resignation? 'I do believe you've said no to me several times this morning already.'

CHAPTER FIVE

BLAKE OPENED HIS mouth to tell her *no* one more time—Joanna or no Joanna—but her phone interrupted them and she turned away, heading back to the lounge chair where she'd left it.

'Crap,' she muttered as she recognised her mother's number on the screen. She did not want to have to deal with her now but, she knew from experience, her mother was best kept on a tight leash. 'I'm sorry, it's my mother,' she apologised to Blake.

Blake gestured with his hands for her to take it then turned back to the sink and his contemplation of London to give them some privacy. Except that was kind of hard in the confines of the boat with her standing just a couple of metres away.

To say Ava sounded strained was an understatement. Even with his back to her he could pick up the tension laced through her words. He hadn't realised how much he'd learned about the subtleties of her voice in three months, which was surprising considering Ava's mother seemed to be doing most of the talking.

He didn't hear Ava say once she was okay or retell the events of last night so from that he had to assume her mother hadn't asked. Ava seemed to be asking her not to do something, her request becoming less and less polite.

Then he heard, 'I'm with…a friend.' And, 'I can't say.'

Then finally, 'I'll fill you in when I get back—just don't give any interviews in the meantime.'

Her mother was going to the press?

There didn't even seem to be a goodbye; he just heard Ava's phone clatter onto the dining table.

When he turned around she was staring out of the window currently flooding in sunlight, her back erect, her messy ponytail even now begging him to pull it out.

'You okay?' he asked.

She turned around slowly and the look on her face was in stark contrast to her self-assurance just prior to the phone call. She looked a lot like she had last night—vulnerable.

'I'm fine,' she dismissed, her voice weary. She lifted a hand and absently rubbed the muscles in her neck. The action caused all sorts of interesting movement inside her shirt. *His* shirt.

Blake kept his gaze firmly trained on her face—he was used to doing that. 'You know, you could have told your mother where you were.'

Ava gave a soft snort. 'Ah...no. She's the last person I would tell.'

Hmm. *Interesting.* 'I take it you two don't get along?'

'You could say that,' Ava said dryly.

'Doesn't she approve of you being a model?'

Ava gave a harsh laugh. 'Oh, no, she approves, all right. She's one of the original pageant queens. The same old story, never quite made it herself so lived out her glory through me. Put me in my first baby competition when I was a month old.'

Blake blinked at the bitterness in her tone. 'Let me guess—you won?'

Ava smiled despite the slight derision in his voice. 'I won every one I ever entered until I was two and my father put his foot down and insisted that I have a *normal* life.'

'But you got back into it later?'

'After Dad died, we were in a lot of debt. Mum worked

really hard doing two jobs to keep the house payments going and then I won a nationwide search for the newest young model and...'

Blake nodded. 'You hit the big time.'

'Yes.'

He frowned. 'So...you two disagreed about the direction of your career?'

'No. Mum hired an agent for me. An old school friend of hers...Paul. He managed every aspect of my career, for those first three years. My jobs, my money, my image. I depended on him for everything—it was him, me and Mum against the world.'

Blake still wasn't sure what the issue was. 'That's... bad?'

'It is when he's embezzling your money behind your back and sleeping with your mother, screwing with her head so even when his treachery was discovered she stood by him, defending him in court, imploring me to give him a second chance, then leaving the country with him *and my money*, marrying him and leaving me, at seventeen, to fend for myself.'

A cold fist pushed up under Blake's diaphragm and he took two steps towards her. How could a mother abandon her teenage daughter like that? 'She chose him over you?'

Ava's lips twisted. It had been a long time since she'd let herself revisit how betrayed, how vulnerable, she'd felt. Dwelling on the past wasn't her thing. But it *had* been a most unusual twelve hours.

'Yes. She did. "You're going to be all right, darling," she said. "You're young and beautiful with contracts lined up out the door thanks to Paul," she said. "I need to be loved too," she said.'

Blake rocked his head from side to side as tension crept into his traps. He finally understood what Ava had meant last night when she'd said she'd learned early not to trust.

She'd been betrayed by two people closest to her—no wonder she was a control freak.

'What happened?'

'They were divorced four years later. Mum came home trying to ingratiate herself but I'd already hired Reggie, who taught me three very important things—trust nobody, *always* control your own money and your agent is *not* your friend.'

Blake made a mental note to apologise to Reggie if they ever met again. He'd obviously armed Ava well in the years since her betrayal. *Maybe a little too well.*

It was a difficult concept for him to wrap his head around. Blake's family were big and loud and intrusive and totally in each other's business and that had been hard to take when all he'd wanted to do was hide away and lick his wounds.

But he'd *never* doubted for a minute that they had his back.

'Our relationship is…strained,' Ava said, her hand dropping from her neck.

'I'm sorry,' he said. 'You should be able to trust family.'

Ava couldn't agree more but sadly, for some people, that wasn't possible. 'Don't be sorry,' she said. 'Just take me with you.'

She sounded so utterly defeated and Blake knew there was no way he could deny her when clearly, despite being surrounded by people, she was pretty much alone in the world. She didn't even have family to lean on, for crying out loud. Her father dead. Her mother abandoning her in favour of her agent.

Her d*on't screw with me* act was just that—an act.

She needed someone she could trust and it looked as if it was going to be him.

A decision that would no doubt come back and bite him hard on the arse.

'Patron, huh?'

It took a second for the meaning of Blake's words to sink in. A spark of hope spluttered to life inside Ava's chest. 'Is that…a yes?'

Blake nodded, her caution so uncharacteristic it only added to his conviction. 'That's a yes.'

Ava felt a rush of relief flow through her veins so hot and hard it was dizzying. She smiled as tension leached from her muscles. Then suddenly, feeling light, feeling that everything was going to be all right, she laughed. Then she gave into temptation, crossing the short distance between them and throwing herself against his chest, her arms around his neck.

'Thank you, thank you,' she said, hugging him hard.

Blake sucked in a breath as the full length of her pressed into the full length of him and he liked how she fitted perfectly. Her ponytail swung a little in his direct vision and he wasn't sure he could survive a few days with it screaming *pull me out, pull me out.*

He shut his eyes. *Safe haven, man.* You're her safe haven.

'Okay, okay. No touchy-feely stuff,' he said, prising her off him, setting her back, but then somewhere out on the street a loud bang cracked the air and she practically leapt back into his arms.

Blake's hands automatically slid onto her waist. 'Hey, it's okay,' he said after a moment or two, the frantic beat of her heart thudding against the wall of his chest as her hands clasped his T-shirt. 'It's just a car backfiring.'

Ava barely heard him over the whoosh of her pulse through her ears but she understood from his non-verbals-his calm, solid presence-that there was no imminent threat. 'Sorry.' She grimaced as she pulled away shakily. 'I'm going to be jumpy for a while.'

Her freckles were standing out again amidst the sudden pallor of her face, the tiny graze on her cheek looking more macabre as Blake's hands slid to her elbows. 'It's fine,' he said, squeezing her gently.

'Thank you,' she murmured, her voice thready.

Blake nodded, his gaze drifting to her mouth before pulling back again. *Not going there.* He took two steps away, putting some distance between them.

'I have conditions,' he said.

It took Ava a few seconds to shake the feeling that the boat had rocked beneath her. And as her mouth tingled she knew it wasn't just from the fright. She cleared her throat.

'Conditions?'

Blake nodded. 'Yes. Two.'

Ava regarded him steadily for a moment. 'Okay then, let's hear them.'

He held up one finger. 'No one knows our location. Not Reggie. Not your PA. Not any of your gal pals. You're supposed to be totally incognito and I'm supposed to be having a peaceful holiday. I don't want it turned into a three-ring circus when someone lets it leak to the paparazzi.'

Ava nodded. She was happy with that—she didn't want her location broadcast either, which was why she hadn't told her mother. 'Fine. I'll let Reggie know we're going away for a few days and—'

'No,' Blake interrupted. 'He knows how to get hold of you. He doesn't need to know you're leaving town.'

'I suppose not.' Ava frowned at him; his indigo eyes were shuttered. 'You don't like him much, do you?'

Blake gave a dismissive shrug of his shoulders. He liked him a lot better now he knew some more about the man. 'The question is do I trust him? And I don't.'

Anyone who was willing to put Ava's career ahead of her protection didn't have her best interests at heart as far as he was concerned. It might make him a great agent but it didn't say a lot for him as a human being.

Ava gave Blake a half-smile. She knew that Reggie came across as utterly money-grubbing but that was why she'd hired him. Her career was the most important thing to

Reggie and he was *exactly* who she'd needed in her corner after sleazoid Paul.

Reggie was all about the business. 'He's the only person I *do* trust.'

In this industry where she trusted no one—she put her faith in Reggie's instincts and his ball-breaking rep. He wouldn't rat her out because he took his client confidentiality seriously—it was his calling card.

Blake thought it was sad that the only person Ava trusted had perpetuated her mistrust of others. 'Well, let's agree to differ on that one,' Blake said.

Ava allowed her smile to become full blown. 'I have a feeling that's going to happen a bit,' she murmured.

Blake grunted. *So did he.* Her smile reached out between them, making her mouth even more appealing, and for a moment he forgot that she'd bribed her way into his life—into his much coveted peaceful holiday. When she looked down her nose at him all haughty it was easy to remember that she was a spoiled prima donna who liked getting her way.

But when she smiled at him like a woman smiling at a man, things got a little hazy.

'Two,' he continued, dragging his mind off her mouth and taking another step back for good measure. 'You have to be in some kind of disguise. There's no point in you coming with me to lie low when you look like—'

Blake paused as his gaze skittered down her body and back up again. His boxers and T-shirt did nothing to disguise her body. Not with her bare shoulder, her hair swinging in a ponytail and legs that went on for ever.

He waved his hand in her general direction. 'That.'

A few months ago Ava would have been insulted at the brief survey of her body and his apparent dismissal. But she knew him well enough now to know that he was just too disciplined to give too much away.

She guessed that was the soldier in him.

She looked down at her body, smoothing her hands down the front to the exposed slice of her belly, which, thanks to a hundred crunches a day and regular visits to the tanning salon, she knew to be flat and toned and tanned and pretty irresistible to most people with a y chromosome and a pulse.

'Like what?' she enquired, looking at him innocently.

Blake gritted his teeth, not fooled by her little performance one iota. 'Like Ava *freaking* Kelly,' he said.

She quirked an eyebrow. 'Should I shave my head?'

Blake gave her a sardonic smile. 'I don't think we need to go quite that extreme. Would hate to incur the wrath of Reggie any more than I have. But maybe a wig? Or definitely hats, something to tuck your hair into. And big dark sunglasses.'

His gaze drifted to those legs again. 'And baggy clothes. No itty-bitty shorts and tiny little T-shirts. *No* red bikinis.' For his own sanity if nothing else. 'No make-up. Nothing that draws attention to you.'

Although he had the feeling she could be wearing a sack and men would still look.

'I don't want some yobo at a pub along the canal recognising you and deciding he can make a quid or two ratting you out to the media. Plain is what we're after,' he said. 'Baggy, too big, shapeless—they are your friends.'

Ava blinked. None of those things had *ever* been her friends. Camouflage wasn't what she did. She spent all her working hours flaunting and flattering her body. 'Well, *gee whiz*, that sounds like fun,' she said, her voice heavy with derision.

But still, she could see his point. People had made a lot of money out of her in the past by tipping off the press. And with the furore that was bound to have been whipped up by last night's incident and her going underground— she'd have a pretty price on her head.

And she couldn't help but wonder what it would be like

to be utterly anonymous, even for a short while. *Not* famous for a few days? She'd been on magazine covers and in the public eye since she was fourteen years old and sometimes she was just so tired of the constant attention and scrutiny.

'They're my conditions.' Blake shrugged. 'Take it or leave it.'

'Take it.' She nodded. She could put up with any fashion sin for a few days. 'Not exactly clothes I have in my closet though.'

Blake shook his head. 'Too unsafe to go there, anyway.' He strode over to the dining table where his mobile was on charge, pleased to be out of range of her in his clothes. 'I'll ring Joanna,' he said. 'We can break the news to her about her windfall, then you can tell her what you need and she can buy it for you then bring it here.'

Ava blinked. 'I can't expect your sister to just drop everything and go clothes shopping for me.'

'Trust me—' he grimaced as the dialling tone sounded in his ear '—when she learns about your generosity, she's going to want to have your babies.'

Finally, almost three hours later, they were under way. The groceries had been delivered and put away. So had the second lot that Ava had ordered when she'd realised how basic the first lot were. And an excitable, starry-eyed Joanna had come and gone. The only people who knew that Ava Kelly was on the boat with Blake were Joanna and Charlie.

And Blake trusted them with his life.

God knew between the two of them they'd practically brought him back from the brink with sheer will power alone. All those days and nights when life hadn't seemed worth living, they'd been there getting him through. Loving him, fighting with him, crying with him, getting drunk with him. Whatever it had taken, they'd done it.

It was slow going through the busy London canal system as he headed west along the Paddington arm of the Grand

Union Canal. Tourists were out enjoying the narrow-boat lifestyle either through private hire or with the many companies that ran canal transport services. The weather was glorious—the sky blue and cloudless, the sun warm, a light breeze ruffling his shirt—and had it not been for his unwanted passenger, it would have been perfect.

Although, to be fair, Ava was exceedingly easy company—so far anyway. Dressed in a pair of baggy shorts that came past her knees and a loose T-shirt with her hair tucked into a cap and dark, saucer-like sunglasses completely obscuring her eyes, she looked like any other tourist standing at the helm. Watching the world go by as she soaked up some rays and intermittently answering half a dozen calls, all from Reggie.

Sure, if someone looked hard enough they'd be able to make out the slenderness of her legs, the erect, model-like way she held herself, the superb bone structure of her heart-shaped face. But at a quick glance she looked as far removed from a supermodel as was possible and no one gawked at her, nudged each other and whispered or pointed their fingers.

She was just another one of them.

Mission: Disguise Ava Kelly, accomplished.

But what surprised him was how much she didn't seem to care. Having braved a rabble of paparazzi most mornings for three months, who she kept sweet with the occasional gourmet snacks and frequent photo opportunities, he'd have thought she'd be missing the limelight already. But she seemed content to rub shoulders with him and make occasional conversation.

Not long after they'd cast off she'd disappeared for a while then reappeared twenty minutes later with two crunchy bread rolls stuffed with ham off the bone, crisp lettuce, a slice of sweet pineapple, seeded mustard and rich mayonnaise. Blake had been hungry but hadn't wanted to waste any more time getting away to stop and eat something, so the food had hit the spot.

'Thanks,' he'd said as he'd licked mayonnaise off his fingers and tried not to notice her doing the same.

'The least I can do is feed you,' she'd said.

And feed him she did. Popping down below every now and then, bringing back blueberry muffins warm from the oven one time and a bowl full of cut fresh strawberries another.

By the time they reached Bulls Bridge it was six in the evening, but with the days still staying light until nine they descended into Brentford via the Hanwell locks.

And Ava proved herself even handier with a windlass. Blake knew that the trip he'd planned out would be slow and physically demanding for one person and he'd been looking forward to the challenge. But having Ava operate the locks while he drove the boat did speed things up considerably.

He held his breath as she chatted with people from other boats at each lock, waiting for the moment of recognition. But it never came and they were mooring along a towpath in Brentford just before eight.

The smell of cooking meat hit Blake twenty minutes later as he stepped inside from making sure the boat was secure and helping the novice narrow-boaters who had pulled their boat up in front of them. His stomach growled at him.

But it was nothing to the growl his libido gave as his eyes fell on a scantily clad Ava shaking her very delectable booty to the music that was obviously filling her ear buds.

The baggy was gone.

She was in a short flimsy gown that fell to mid-thigh and seemed to cling to every line and curve of her body from the hem north—it certainly clung lovingly to every contour of her butt. It was tied firmly at the waist, which was just as well as she sang along, in a truly terrible falsetto, and stirred something in a bowl.

Ava Kelly might have excelled at a lot of things but singing was not one of them.

Her hair was wet and down. Her feet were bare.

The supermodel was back.

After standing gawping like an idiot for a moment or two he moved closer and cleared his throat to get her attention.

Ava looked up from the dressing she was mixing. 'Oh, sorry.' She grinned, pulling the ear buds out. 'This song always gets me going. Are you hungry? I'm cooking steak. Plus I think this is probably *the* most divine salad dressing—' she dipped her finger in and rolled her eyes in obvious pleasure '—I've ever made.'

A dark drop of the balsamic-looking liquid landed on her chest, just above the criss-cross of her gown at her cleavage and, God help him, Blake's gaze followed it down. She scooped it up quickly but not before he'd taken note of unfettered breasts. Not a line or a strap mark visible through the clinging fabric of the gown.

He looked back at her face. Hell yeh. He was hungry all right.

Freaking starving.

'I thought we'd eat at the pub up the tow path,' he said.

'Tomorrow,' she dismissed, waving her hand and turning back to the job at hand. 'If you want to have a shower, you have six minutes until these babies are ready.'

Blake shook his head. He was going to need much more than six minutes to calm himself down—even in a cold shower. He'd settle for alcoholic fortification instead.

'Drink?' he asked as he opened the fridge and grabbed the long neck of a boutique beer, twisted the lid off and took a long deep pull.

Ava looked up, watching the movement of his throat as he swallowed. There was something very primal about a man guzzling beer. She wondered what he'd do if she sauntered over and slicked her tongue up the hard ridge of his trachea.

She looked back at the steaks cooking in the pan. 'I'll have one of those, thanks.'

Blake cocked an eyebrow. 'Beer. *You* drink beer?' he said as he pulled one out for her and cracked the lid.

Ava heard the surprise bordering on derision in his voice and looked at him. 'Yes. Why? What do you think I drink?'

'Wheatgrass smoothies,' he said, remembering how she often came home from somewhere in her shrink-wrapped gym gear slurping on something disgustingly green.

She took the beer from him. 'Not when I'm relaxing.'

Blake leaned against the fridge. 'Champagne? Fruity cocktails? Dirty cowboys…or whatever the hell those shots are called that women seem to like to knock back in bars these days.'

Ava laughed. He didn't sound as if he approved. 'I like champagne and fruity cocktails, sure. But underneath it all, I'm just a pint-of-beer girl.'

Blake snorted in disbelief.

But, just to prove him wrong, she tipped back her head and took three very long, somehow very erotic, swallows. His gaze drifted down her undulating neck, to her breasts again—not too big, not too small and extremely perky— then back up. She was smiling at him with that knowing little half-smile of hers, her eyelids shuttered, when his gaze returned to her face.

Ava's pulse skipped a beat as their gazes locked for long moments. Heat bloomed to her belly and breasts, making them feel heavy and tight. She toyed with the neck of the bottle, running her fingers up and down the frosty glass as their stare continued.

After three months of scrupulous politeness, he was finally looking at her. Really looking at her.

And there was a *very* definite vibe between them.

'You shouldn't judge a book by its cover, Blake,' she murmured.

Blake sucked in a breath as her voice broke the connection between them. Her cover had sure fallen away fast these last twenty-four hours since being shot at. And he wasn't sure he liked the unpredictable woman in front of him. At least he knew who the other Ava was.

'I'll set the table,' he said, turning away, grateful for something to occupy his mind and his hands.

Other than putting them all over her.

CHAPTER SIX

AVA WAS STARVING by the time they sat down to juicy steaks, a fresh green salad and warm rolls from the oven complete with garlic butter she'd whipped up.

'Where'd you learn to cook?' Blake asked as he bit into his steak. His groan of satisfaction caused a spike in her pulse and a pull in her belly that was entirely sexual.

She shrugged. 'My dad. He was a chef. My earliest memories were being in the kitchen cooking with him. It was our thing we did together. I think I learned through osmosis.'

Blake quirked an eyebrow. 'You said he died?'

Ava nodded. 'When I was twelve. Heart attack.'

Blake watched as the drying strands of her hair glided over each other, the caramel burnished to toffee beneath the expensive down lights. 'That must have been hard.'

Ava nodded. He didn't know the half of it. 'Emotionally and financially. He had his own restaurant, which was almost bankrupt. It was a tough time...'

Blake could tell she didn't want to elaborate on the subject of her father any more and he didn't push as he shifted the conversation to their route tomorrow. He understood. He was a private person too, he wouldn't want a virtual stranger prying into his personal business either.

The army shrink had been bad enough.

But it wasn't what he'd expected from her. From what

he'd witnessed these last few months she seemed to live so much of her life as an open book. In a goldfish bowl. It had been easy—and far preferable—to think of her as a *brand*, a *product*. As *Ava Kelly, Inc.* instead of a flesh and blood woman.

Except for the last twenty-four hours. Sleeping in his bed, cooking in his kitchen, dancing at his sink.

In her gown.

Her very short, very clingy gown.

Ava slid out of the booth and picked up their plates after they'd finished eating.

'Leave them,' Blake said, also standing. 'I'll do them.'

'I don't mind,' Ava said. She was very aware that she'd hijacked his holiday, completely disregarding his plans and inserting herself into the middle of them. The least she could do was make herself useful. She didn't want Blake to think that her jet-set lifestyle had made her too big for her boots—she didn't expect to be waited on.

He grabbed the plates. 'You cook, I clean. House rules.'

Ava resisted for a moment, holding onto the edges as he pulled them towards him, dragging her in close to him, just two dinner plates separating them. She became aware again of *the vibe*. It hummed between them, filling each breath with his essence, enervating each heartbeat with anticipation. What would he do if she just leaned in and kissed him? That was the beauty of being tall—she didn't even have to go up on tippy-toes. His mouth was right there, level with hers.

'*Boat* rules,' she murmured.

Blake swallowed as she looked down her nose to his mouth, lingering there for a moment before returning to his eyes. He had no doubt she was thinking about kissing him and he quelled a sudden urge to lick his lips for fear of what it might give away.

Or encourage.

She seemed to sway a little closer and he quelled his next urge—to do a little kissing himself—too. Instead he gave a brief smile and took a step back, the plates transferring easily to his hands. 'Boat rules,' he agreed briskly.

Ava blinked as he turned away from her and headed to the sink, gathering wits that had taken up residence somewhere south of her belly button. She'd been sure he'd been about to kiss her.

So why hadn't he?

Was he one of those guys who got a little stage fright when it came to kissing her? Intimidated by her being a *supermodel*? Performance anxiety? Funny, he hadn't struck her as the type. She'd have thought the whole good-with-his-hands thing would translate to the bedroom.

'Okay, fine,' she said, finally finding her voice. 'Your boat, your rules. Knock yourself out.' She looked around the saloon, for a distraction, her gaze falling on the television. 'Would you think me terribly vain if I turned the news on and see what they're saying about me?'

Blake shook his head—anything was preferable to her standing there, her gaze boring into the back of his head. 'Nope. Remote on top of the telly,' he said. 'I'll make us a coffee.'

Because staying awake all night on a caffeine high thinking about nearly kissing her in a gown that should have come with a highly flammable label was just what he needed.

Not.

Ava tucked her legs up underneath her as she flipped through the channels till she found some news. Apart from updates from Reggie concerning her situation, she'd been out of touch with the big wide world for twenty-four hours. And it was good to get engrossed in something other than Blake's big brooding presence.

By the time he joined her fifteen minutes later she was

reasonably absorbed in the news. He passed her a mug and was just settling himself into the other chair when a segment on her was introduced. There was nothing new—no arrests, no suspects, just speculation as the events were recounted. And a little air of mystery as the anchor woman speculated as to Ava's whereabouts now that the famous model had *gone underground*.

There was footage of her house and brief glimpses of her last night in the back of an ambulance as well as loads of file footage of her strutting catwalks, shooting a commercial and her smiling at the gaggle of paparazzi as she left her house, patiently moving through them as they surrounded her.

Blake shook his head at the rabble, half of the photographers walking backwards—completely hazardous—to ring every last photo op out of her. 'I don't know how you do that every day,' he said.

Ava shrugged. 'You get used to it.'

Blake shuddered. 'I couldn't live like that, with every minute of my life on show, a camera in my face.'

'It's okay,' Ava said, swivelling the chair to face him as the segment finished and the anchor starting talking about a string of break and enters. 'I've had a camera in my face since I was fourteen so...' She took a sip of her coffee. 'You just make boundaries,' she said. 'Outside I'm public property, inside I'm off-limits.'

Blake thought that sounded like a fairly limited right to privacy. 'But aren't there days you just want to tell them to—?' He stopped himself short of the phrase he would have used had it been him and Charlie talking.

'Do something anatomically impossible to themselves?' she suggested.

Blake chuckled. 'Yes.'

Ava sighed. The sort of life she led was hard for everyday people to understand. 'I *have* to court them, Blake. I'm twenty-seven years old. That's bloody *ancient* in the circles I move in. *And* I'm getting older every day. The paparazzi, the press…they keep me current, keep me in the hearts and minds of people. Good press, good image equals strong interest. One day soon the interest, the jobs, will dry up but until then Reggie says the paps can make you or break you.'

Blake snorted. 'Your agent is a shark.'

'Yeh.' She grinned. 'That's why I hire him. Someone who's sole job it is in life to look after my career. He does it well. I wouldn't be where I am today without him.'

Blake rolled his eyes. 'Oh, please, you make him sound like he's some saint doing it out of the goodness of his heart. I'm sure he's being more than adequately compensated.'

'Absolutely,' she confirmed as she absently traced the hem of her gown where it draped against her thigh with her index finger. 'He's doing it for his fifteen per cent. But at least *that's* an honest business transaction. Telling the difference was a very hard-earned lesson for me.'

Blake heard the sudden steel in her voice and was reminded again that for all her privilege Ava hadn't exactly had it easy. His gaze dropped to where her finger was doodling patterns on her hemline. With her legs tucked up under her, the gown had ridden up some more until it was sitting high on her thighs. It covered what it needed with a little to spare but that still left a whole lot of long, golden leg on display.

Legs he'd managed not to look at or think about for three months. Legs that he was fast developing a fascination with.

She looked at him then and he dragged his gaze back to her face with difficulty. 'Have you thought about what you're going to do after?' It was the first thing that came into his head that didn't involve her legs. 'When the jobs dry up?'

She shook her head as her finger stroked and swirled.

'Not really. I won't *have* to do anything. I'm financially secure. I have the perfume line I'm launching and Reggie's always fielding offers from media and fashion to keep me busy. But I don't know,' she said, shaking her head. 'I've been modelling since I was fourteen…I *honestly* don't really know anything else.'

Her finger stopped tracing as she looked at him speculatively. 'What about you? Did you have some exit strategy for leaving the army?' Her gaze dropped to his leg then back to his face again. 'Were you…prepared?'

Blake grunted. 'No.' Certainly not prepared for the way he'd left. 'I was a career soldier. Never thought about getting out.'

Something shimmered in her eyes that looked a lot like connection as she lazily swivelled the chair back and forth. He couldn't remember ever having a conversation with a woman like this—apart from his shrink. Ever really wanting to—*including his shrink*.

He hated those conversations.

But, for some reason, it felt as if Ava was in a unique position to truly understand—looking down the barrel of shortened career prospects.

'What *did* you do?' she asked.

Blake looked down at his left leg. 'Spent a load of time in hospitals of one description or another.' High-dependency wards, surgical wards, rehab wards. Surgeon's offices, prosthetic offices, shrink's offices.

He could feel the intensity of her gaze on his face as he stared at his leg. Feel it like an invisible bloom of heat swelling in his peripheral vision.

'I meant after that…?'

She said it so softly, Blake had to turn his head to catch it. *A mistake*. Her finger had stopped its hypnotic path but her gown clung, her hair was now dry, her mouth was soft and, for some inexplicable reason—maybe it was sharing last night's frightening episode—he felt he could talk to her. He'd spent three months avoiding it. Avoiding talking to her about anything other than the reno and her haughty demands.

But she seemed different now. Vulnerable, stripped back, human. Like a woman. Not a brand.

'Well, let me see…I spent the first six months with my head up my arse feeling sorry for myself, consuming large amounts of alcohol and pissing off just about everybody who knew and loved me.' He grimaced. 'I wouldn't recommend you do that.'

Ava smiled. 'Check.'

'Then I got a phone call—' He stopped himself before he went any further.

He'd only ever told the shrink this stuff. And while he felt some weird kind of kinship with her he just couldn't go there. Prior to last night he'd been hard put sharing with her something as basic as his relationship with Joanna. Now, twenty-four hours later he was ready to spill his guts?

It was confusing and he didn't like it.

He raked a hand through his hair. 'Let's just say I got some…news—' news that had shocked him to the core '—and I realised that there *were* worse things than having one leg and that it was time to stop acting like the only person in the world who'd ever had something bad happen to them and get on with it.'

'And that's when you and Charlie formed the company?'

'No.' Blake shook his head. 'That's when I bought this boat.' He looked around the interior. 'I spent a year fixing her up. Stripping her right back and rebuilding her from the hull up.'

He gave a self-deprecating smile. 'Manual work can be quite therapeutic.'

'I can imagine.' An image of Blake in a tool belt as he'd worked on her kitchen bench rose in her mind. Would he have taken his shirt off when he'd been working in the hull of the boat?

He nodded. 'Lots of things to tear down and rip out. Lots of pounding and hammering and loud noisy power tools.'

Ava laughed at the note of relish in his voice. 'Be still my beating heart.'

Blake found himself laughing too. 'It's a guy thing.'

'I'm guessing.' She grinned. 'So…your brother saw what a great job you'd done here and you decided to start the company?'

'No. It evolved out of another company, that Charlie had started five years before that. I was doing some labouring for him in between doing up the boat.' He paused. 'Charlie and Joanna were determined to keep me busy…' He grimaced. 'And then, because I have an engineering background, I helped out with some design things and the company was really starting to take off, but it needed a cash injection to get across the line so he offered me a partnership.'

Ava let it all sink in. So not only was he a war hero but he was an engineer who could design stuff and was so good with his hands he could make his own designs too.

Clearly, he had plenty to fall back on.

'Wow.' She blinked. 'Somehow, despite what most would call an *exceedingly* successful life, you've just made me feel completely inadequate. All I know how to do is wear clothes.'

Blake chuckled at her blatant self-deprecation. 'Hey.' He smiled. 'People need clothes.'

She shot him a quelling look. They both knew people didn't need clothes a person had to earn six figures to afford. 'I'm going to be totally screwed when the next big thing pushes me off my pedestal.'

Blake laughed again. There was something very sexy about profanity coming from her posh mouth. 'Don't be discouraged. I hear they love ex-celebrities for those reality television shows the world can't seem to get enough of.'

Ava shuddered. 'No, thanks. I'm not going on any bug-infested island where I have to pee in a hole in the ground and build my own shelter.' She took in his big broad shoulders and those capable hands. 'Not without you anyway.' Although now the idea was out there it might be worth it to watch Blake in his natural element. Maybe with his shirt off?

A soft fizz warmed her belly as her gaze made it back to his face. 'Sorry.' She lifted and dropped a shoulder in a half-shrug. 'I just can't imagine me there, can you?'

Blake sobered as he followed the movement and the ripple effect it had across her chest. Her breasts jiggled slightly, the fabric clinging to them moulded the movement to perfection. He tore his gaze away, met her knowing eyes.

Crap.

'Before today, no,' he said, ploughing on, determined not to acknowledge either his perving or her awareness of it. 'But I've been impressed with how very unpretentious you've been today. There's been no hissy fit over the cut on your face or hand. No hysteria about career-ending scars. No sitting on your butt expecting to be waited on. You got in and helped *and*—' his gaze flicked briefly to her legs then back again '—current attire excepted, you disguised yourself just as I asked. I know bagging up couldn't have been easy for you, but you did *and* you were very generous about it.'

Pleasure at his praise flooded warmth through her system and heat to areas where pleasure meant an entirely different thing. She wasn't sure why *his* praise meant anything to her. She lived in a world that sung her praises daily—and she pretty much took that for granted. She certainly wasn't looking for more. Certainly not from him.

Maybe it was because he'd been so hard to engage during those three months he'd spent at her house? Ava was used to male attention, hell, she *loved* male attention and generally took it as her due. But there'd been a very definite line between them that *he'd* drawn in thick black marker.

Nothing personal had crossed between them.

He'd been polite and respectful, prompt with her queries and had kept his eyes firmly trained on her face. He'd been one hundred per cent professional, resisting slipping into an easier, more casual relationship she'd tried to establish.

Always holding himself back.

She hadn't been able to break through his reserve. And that had been frustrating, galling and intriguing all at once.

But these last twenty-four hours had seen that line disappear. And here he was actually praising her.

Even checking her out.

She wondered how much further she could take it. It could be fun to find out, to push him a little. Discover his buttons. They were both adults and the night was theirs. She smiled at him as she stroked her palm down her neck to her chest, three fingers finding their way under the lapel of the gown.

'It's a lot easier to be baggy on the outside when you're spoiling yourself underneath it all and there's nothing quite like sexy underwear to make you feel sexy all over no matter what you're wearing,' she said.

Blake frowned. Was she saying what he thought she was saying?

'Joanna agreed,' Ava added. 'She didn't think I should have to let myself go altogether.'

'I bet she did,' he said. His sister was always on some mission to set him up. *But Ava freaking Kelly was way out of his league.*

She ought to know he'd had enough drama in his life without inviting a diva in.

'And,' Ava continued, 'I have to say, she has a real eye for classy lingerie. Not that I have any of it on right now.'

Blake tried and failed not to follow the stroke of her fingers as they played with the lapel. Her fingers rubbed along the edge of the fabric, lifting it slightly, exposing a little more flesh to his view.

The air grew thick between them and Ava sensed that the time was ripe to make a move. It didn't faze her. She knew what she wanted and she had the confidence to go after it.

Some people called that bold. She called it decisive.

'I've been thinking,' she said, her gaze firmly trained on his face, 'about the sleeping arrangements tonight.'

She stopped. Waited. He wasn't objecting. Wasn't bolting. He was watching, intently, his eyes on her hand.

'I don't think it's fair that you should give up your bed for me again and so I thought…maybe we could…share…?'

Those words finally did the trick, dragging Blake's head back from the edge and his eyes back from her cleavage.

Was she…propositioning him?

'You mean…you lie on one side with your head at the top and I lie on the other with my head at the bottom and we both get a good night's sleep?'

Ava shook her head. 'Nope.'

The secret little smile playing at the edges of her mouth, the way she looked down her nose at him with blatant sexual interest, did strange things to Blake's equilibrium. It was just as well he was sitting down.

She *was* propositioning him.

There was nothing touch-me-not about this Ava. This Ava was very, very touchable.

Blake's heart rate slowed right down in his chest as blood rushed south. His brain might be saying no but other parts of him weren't listening. Ava Kelly was trouble with a capital T. And he'd had more than enough trouble to last him a lifetime. Being a supermodel's plaything for a night or two might be every man's wet dream but his doom receptors were working overtime.

'I…don't think that would be such a good idea,' he said.

Ava blinked. Not the response she was used to. *Frankly she thought it was the best idea she'd had in a long time.*

But Blake *had* spent three months keeping his distance and she already knew he was the strong, serious, cautious type.

Well, she didn't get to the top of her game by taking no for an answer and she sure as hell wasn't going to tonight either.

'Okay.' She placed her coffee mug on the coffee table and stood. She walked the three paces that separated their chairs until the outside of her right thigh was brushing the outside of his. She looked down at him.

'I know this isn't what we planned. And I know this isn't the kind of relationship you and I have had to this point. But I'm just going to put this out there.'

Ava's pulse fluttered madly and her breathing sped up as she lifted her right leg to step over his thighs, placing them between her legs. He shifted in his chair and she shut her eyes briefly as the denim scraped erotically against the sensitive inner flesh of her bare thighs.

When she opened them again his indigo gaze was staring straight at the knot of her belt as if he was trying to undo it through mind power alone. Heat flared behind her belly button and tingled at the juncture of her thighs.

'I'm attracted to you, Blake,' she said. 'I think you're attracted to me. We have tonight…maybe a few nights on this boat together and we're both adults. I'm just saying… we could have some fun. That wouldn't be such a bad thing, right?'

Right. Blake knew she was right. He had no problems with two consenting adults having a little fun together. He used to indulge in quite a lot of *fun* before the explosion. But since…

Sure, there'd been women but *fun* didn't really fit into his vocabulary these days. Sex was a lot of things—communication, connection, stress relief. An activity engaged in to relieve a build-up of testosterone.

Pleasurable. Enjoyable. Necessary. But not fun.

Because having fun felt wrong.

'Blake?'

He was still staring at that knot and she could tell he was teetering on the edge. She reached for it then, slowly worked at it with fingers that shook just a little until it slid loose and the belt fell to her sides. The two front edges of the gown slid over each other parting slightly.

She was still covered—barely.

Blake swallowed against a throat that felt as dry as the desert. His erection surged against his jeans and the urge to open her gown, to see more than a glimpse of cleavage, thrummed through his system like the steady backbeat of a tropical downpour. He glanced up at her to tell her to step away but her cat eyes looked back at him, her mouth parted.

He sucked in a breath and curled his fingers into the lounge beside him. 'Hell, Ava.'

Ava felt dizzy from the longing in his low husky growl and she squeezed her legs hard against his to stay grounded.

'I've shocked you, haven't I? I'm sorry. Not very lady-like I guess. I've always been a little too forthright for my own good.'

Blake snorted as her posh ladylike voice made excuses for her brazen proposal. In the grand scheme of shocking, it barely rated as a blip. 'I don't give a rat's arse for lady-like,' he growled.

He liked a *woman* between the sheets, not some snooty *lady* who was worried about getting her hair messed up.

Ava might talk a little on the posh side and have that haughty little look of hers well rehearsed but her frank proposition, the way she'd thrown her leg over him just now, the sureness of her fingers as she'd undone her belt, told him she was no *lady* in the bedroom.

'Well, okay then,' Ava said, smiling down at him. Their gazes locked and she waited for him to reach for her, to make the first move. *Or the next one, anyway.* But she could still see a glimmer of that famous reserve, that wariness in his eyes.

Surely he wasn't…intimidated? Blake didn't strike her as the kind of guy that needed his hand held, but if that was what was required…

CHAPTER SEVEN

AVA SMILED AT him encouragingly. 'It's okay, you know,' she said, 'to be a little…daunted. It's really quite common. Some guys are a little freaked out at first because of who I am… They don't want to screw it up and it makes them… nervous…reticent. But really, I'm just a woman.'

She leaned forward, conscious of her gown gaping a little more and the lowering of his gaze. She picked up his hand, and placed it halfway up her thigh.

'A flesh and blood woman,' she continued. 'Don't think of me as a…celebrity. I'm just Ava…a woman just like any other.'

Blake's gaze stayed fixed on where his hand met her flesh as Ava straightened. Her thigh was warm beneath his palm. And very, very female. Something his erection appreciated with gusto. So much that it almost made him forget her ridiculous statement.

Lord. Her ego sure as hell hadn't been scared into submission last night.

She didn't *intimidate* him.

But she definitely got under his skin.

He dropped his hand from her thigh before he did something completely contradictory like smoothing it up. All the way up. He looked up instead—a much safer alternative—as he mentally thrust the temptation aside.

'No, Ava.'

Ava heard the roughness of longing in his voice despite his denial. What *was* his problem? And then suddenly something else occurred to her and she felt both stupid and insensitive. Throwing herself at him—an *injured* war veteran.

'Oh, God, I'm so sorry,' she whispered. 'Your injuries...' She shook her head. 'I should have thought. I didn't realise you couldn't...that you can't...that you're...impotent... I'm so sorry...'

Blake almost choked at her wild assumption. Right at this second he'd never been more bloody potent in his life.

Or more goaded into proving it.

'Screw it,' he growled, forgetting all the reasons he shouldn't as he grabbed her hand and yanked.

Ava barely had a chance to catch her breath before she landed hard in his lap, looming over him, her thighs straddling his. Her gown had flown open and her bare breasts grazed the neckline of his shirt. Her hands clutched for purchase, finding the hard wall of muscle that constituted his chest.

But she didn't protest or stop to clarify. She just followed her instincts. And her instincts led her to his mouth. A mouth that was seeking hers, his fingers spearing into her hair, his hands dragging her head down to his.

Her mouth down to his.

And when his lips touched hers, full and firm and open, she opened to him too, parting instantly, her nostrils full of the intoxicating scent of him, her tongue savouring the hint of beer and the fuller, earthier taste of aroused man.

His hand slid over her hip to the small of her back, his palm pressing hard against her, and her belly contracted. He slid it up, following the furrow of her spine, and she shivered. He trekked it around to her front, filling his palm with the soft flesh of her breast, squeezing and rubbing his finger across the turgid peak of her nipple, and she arched her back and moaned, 'Blake,' against his mouth.

His other hand slid to her butt cheek and squeezed and she couldn't think for the bombardment of sensations. For the smell of him filling her head. The taste of him consuming her senses. She just needed more.

To be closer, nearer. To imprint herself. To feel him around her.

To feel him inside her.

She couldn't remember ever wanting a man as desperately as she wanted Blake. Men and sex came easy to her and Blake's resistance had been a challenge. But this wasn't triumph she was feeling. This was purely sexual. Blake gave and gave and gave—plundering, stroking, kneading, touching—and she wanted everything he had to offer.

She squirmed against him, signalling a need she was too far gone to ask for. And that was when she became aware of it. A hardness beneath her right thigh. A flatness. Not like his other thigh that had the flexibility of hot flesh over steely muscle. There was no give there. Just rigidity. And a very definite edge. *His prosthesis.*

But then he was yanking her hips forward, bringing her in contact with more flesh on steel. Something hard and long and very, very potent. Making her forget everything else. She tried to move, to obey the dictates of her body, to grind down on him, to feel every inch of his erection, but he held her there, both hands clamped on her butt now, kissing her deeper, wilder, wetter.

'Blake,' she muttered against his mouth as she tried to squirm, to rub herself shamelessly along the length of him.

Blake groaned as he held her fast. He'd only meant this as a demonstration of his capabilities but it was careening out of his control. Her mouth tasted like beer and sin and he wanted to taste her all over. He hadn't bargained for how perfect she'd feel in his hands. How she'd melt into him, all her can't-touch-this veneer evaporating.

Or how very much he'd been denying himself.

Ava Kelly was one hell of a woman and telling himself she was technically still a client and a pain-in-the-butt one to boot just wasn't going to cut it now his erection had taken control.

He wanted to get her naked, he wanted to get her horizontal; he wanted to get her under him. His head was full of her throaty whimpers, his hands were full of her flesh, his mouth was full of her taste but it still wasn't enough.

Her hand found his erection then and he moaned as she palmed it, pressing himself into her hand. His zip fell away beneath her questing fingers and then she was reaching inside his underwear, freeing him, her palm hot against him as she squeezed his girth.

Blake broke off the kiss on a guttural groan, his eyes practically rolling back in his head as he dragged in much-needed air. Her forehead pressed against his and he opened his eyes to the delectable sight of her breasts swaying hypnotically, the light pink nipples darker now as they formed two hard points.

With her hair falling around them in a curtain and the only sound between them the thick rasp of their breath, it was as if they were the only two people in the world. Far away from the world of Ava Kelly and her entourage. Which was just as well with her hand getting so intimately acquainted with his freed erection.

He shut his eyes as she wrapped her hand around him and started to smooth it up and down the length of him.

'God, you're so *freaking* hard,' she whispered into the space between them. 'I knew there was a reason I'd put my trust in you.'

The words were like a bucket of cold water and Blake froze, his eyes snapping open.

Trust.

She had to use *that* word?

He looked down at himself, at her hand on him. *What the hell was he doing?*

God, how had this got so out of hand? He was only supposed to be proving he could get it up, not demonstrating its full working capabilities. Having sex with Ava was a bad idea and her being practically naked with a hand full of his erection didn't make it any less so.

Every instinct he owned—prior to five minutes ago— had told him to stay away, and he would do well to remember that.

She *trusted* him, for God's sake.

The woman had so few people in the world to put her faith in and he was taking advantage of her sucky situation.

'Stop…wait,' he said, shifting in the chair, covering her hand with his, grateful when she stopped the mindlessly good stroking.

Ava frowned, her hand stilling. Her head spun from the sexual buzz, her brain already someplace else where he felt good and hard inside her. 'Wha…?' she said, pulling away slightly.

'Just…no…hop up…' he said. 'Let me up.'

Blake struggled to get up, trying to displace her safely and stand himself without falling in a heap. Ava stood there looking confused, her gown open, her body flushed and lovely, and he turned away to dispel the image, to block it from his sight.

'Blake?'

He felt a hundred kinds of idiot at her plaintive query as he tucked his protesting erection in and zipped himself up. His breathing was still all bent out of shape and he raked a hand through his hair as he took a moment to gather himself.

When he turned back he was grateful she'd done up her gown. But she'd gone from looking confused and unsure to pretty pissed off.

Not that he could blame her. His erection knew exactly how she felt.

'I'm sorry,' he said. 'I shouldn't have started that… I

was trying to prove that everything was in full working order. I just got a little…carried away.'

Ava glared at him. 'You think?'

'I'm sorry,' he repeated. Because what else could he say?

Ava tried to wrap her head around what had just transpired. 'I don't understand,' she said. 'What happened?'

Blake took a steadying breath. 'I don't want to do this.'

Ava snorted. 'You wanted it all right. You wanted it when you kissed me, you wanted it when you touched me and you sure as hell wanted it when I had my hand in your pants.'

Blake had to concede she made some very good points. 'Of course my *body* wants you,' he said. 'I'm a man and you're one of the most beautiful women on the planet and, as you pointed out before, we're attracted to each other. But I'm thirty-three years old, Ava, not some horny teenager who can't control himself. My brain's telling me this is a stupid thing to do.'

Ava gave another snort. 'That's not what your erection was telling me.'

'Yeh, well…' he raked a hand through his hair '…erections tend to be fairly unreliable indicators of what a man should and shouldn't do.'

'Well, at least they're honest,' she said vehemently. 'At least they tell it like it is. I know you wanted me right now, Blake, and I don't know why you're pretending you don't, why you're pretending it's a bad thing. We're just two human beings coming together, finding a little pleasure together. It's really not that complicated.'

Blake was struck suddenly by how spoiled she was sounding. He'd forgotten how irritating that was in the last twenty-four hours. Obviously she'd pegged him as a sure thing and she wasn't impressed with being knocked back. Clearly she was used to getting her way sexually too.

He half expected to see her stamp her foot.

'Is it *so* hard to believe that someone doesn't want to have sex with you?'

Ava heard the underlying disbelief in his question and it made her crankier. 'Frankly, yes.' Men wanted her—always had. And she'd taken her pick.

Blake almost laughed as her haughty look came back and, even barely dressed in a clingy gown, she managed to look imperious. 'Oh, my God, you've never been knocked back, have you?'

Ava gave a very definitive shake of her head. 'Nope.'

Blake did laugh this time. He'd always had a fairly high success rate with women, even since the explosion. But part of becoming a man, in his opinion, was realising that not every woman was going to think you were sex on a stick.

And it was how a guy took that news that separated the boys from the men.

'Well, welcome to the *real* world,' he said.

Ava *did not* think any of this was funny. She still felt jittery as her cells came down from their sexual high without the satisfaction they craved. 'Oh, I see,' she said, putting her hand on her hip. 'This is some kind of life lesson for me, is it?'

Blake should have been astounded by her egocentricity but nothing about her surprised him any more. 'You know, Ava, this may come as a surprise, but not everything is about you.'

Ava ignored his derisive put down in favour of getting to the bottom of a situation she'd never been in before. 'So… let me get this straight. You're attracted to me but you don't want to have sex with me?'

Blake smiled at her obvious confusion. 'Oh, I want to, all right. I'm just not going to.'

Ava stared at him. Well, now she was totally lost. Why not take what you wanted, especially when it was on offer? 'But…why not?'

Blake shook his head. She really had no clue about the

real world. She was so used to getting her way and taking what she wanted from life, because she could, that she never stopped to think that some things were better off left alone.

'Because it's a whole lot of complicated for a few lousy nights, Ava.'

Ava folded her arms. 'There would be *nothing* lousy about them.'

Blake smiled at her snooty self-assurance. 'I'm sure you're right,' he conceded. If she did other things even half as well as she kissed he was doomed.

'So what's the problem?'

He sighed. Obviously she needed it spelled out. 'I'm supposed to be offering you safe harbour, Ava, not taking advantage of you.'

As a British soldier his uniform had been a symbol of security and he'd always taken that seriously. It just didn't feel right somehow to violate the trust she'd put in him. Just because he hadn't asked for it, didn't mean he was going to mess with it.

'And that would make perfect sense if I was here rocking in a corner and jumping at shadows like some little scared mouse. But *I'm* coming on to *you*. I think consent to take advantage of me is implied. So what else have you got?'

Blake pushed a hand through his hair at her casual dismissal of values he held dear.

God, she was irritating.

'How about, I don't like women who are spoiled and self-centred no matter how beautiful they are or how good they look naked. It's not an attractive quality and I'm not some guy who'll turn a blind eye to that just to get laid. I don't want to be your distraction of choice while you're *slumming it* on a canal boat. I'm not some plaything for a rich woman to amuse herself with.'

Ava blinked at his unflattering appraisal of her. Okay, she might be used to getting her own way but she wasn't a complete egomaniac either. She didn't regard him as a *plaything*. She just saw a situation they could both have a little fun with.

'I don't see you like that,' she said, dropping her arms until they wrapped around her waist. 'This isn't me being bored or spoiled either. I just don't see why we should deny ourselves when we both want this.'

'Well, I guess in your hedonistic world you wouldn't,' he said. 'But I learned a few years ago to stay away from things that can blow up in your face and, lady, you have highly explosive written all over you.'

Ava knew that he hadn't meant to flatter her but she was anyway. She was so used to being described as cool and snooty. The media had dubbed her *Keep-Away Kelly* when she'd really hit the big time because of the aloofness she'd worked so hard to cultivate.

It was her point of difference and she'd worked it.

To be told she was the opposite was strangely thrilling. 'Thank you.'

Blake rolled his eyes. 'It wasn't a compliment.'

Ava grinned at his terse exasperation. 'I know. Which strangely only makes me want you more.'

Blake shook his head. There wasn't much else that could be said here. He was determined to keep things between them strictly platonic. She seemed determined to do the opposite.

Ken Biddle had better catch his man quick. *Before Ava caught hers.*

'I'm going to bed,' he said.

Ava watched him turn away, admiring the back view of him as he veered to the left and headed down the corridor, presumably for the bathroom. His limp was barely discernible. 'You should know I don't give up so easily,' she called.

Blake felt her silky threat—or was that a promise?—land on target right between his shoulder blades. 'I'll consider myself warned,' he said, without turning around, then stepped gratefully into the bathroom and shut the door.

He leaned against it heavily, gripping the door handle hard, trying to get control of a groin that had leaped to life again at her sexy warning. His hand brushed something and he looked down to find a scrap of black lace in the shape of a bra.

He groaned as he pulled it off, and held it up in front of him, letting it dangle from his index finger. Pink ribbon weaved along the cup edges delineated them and a little pink bow at the cleavage, complete with diamanté, winked out at him. His groin went from aching to throbbing.

This was the sort of stuff she was going to be wearing under her clothes?

Fabulous.

He hung it back where he found it then pulled out his mobile from his pocket, scrolling to Joanna's number and hitting 'message'.

Thx heaps 4 the lingerie you meddler.

He hit send and waited where he was for the few seconds it took to get a reply. The phone vibrated in his hand and he read the screen. *Thought you might like.*

Blake tapped a reply. *I don't.*

A few more seconds. *OK. Sure. Keep forgetting you are the *only* man on earth not born with the lingerie gene.*

Blake shook his head. *Don't Joanna. Not going there.*

Joanna's *Uh-huh* reply rankled.

I'm not.

The reply came swiftly. *Uh-huh.*

He grimaced as his fingers flew across the touch pad. *God you're irritating. I should have let Charlie strap you to the front of his bike when you were 2.*

Blake waited for the reply. And waited. He was about to give up and get into the shower when his phone vibrated in his hand again. Four words that hit like a sledgehammer.

What would Colin say???

Blake bumped his head back against the door. Low blow. His mate would think he'd lost his mind for just having turned down an invitation to heaven with one of the world's most nicely put-together women.

Another vibration. *He's dead. You're alive. So live.*

Blake hated it when Joanna played on his guilt over Colin. And she knew it. *I definitely should have let Charlie use u as a human bumper bar.*

A smiley face appeared on the screen. *Love you 2. Night xxx.*

Blake shoved his phone back in his pocket, pushing aside the unsettled feelings that both Ava and Joanna had roused. He shucked off his clothes and moved into the large glass shower recess. One of the beauties of a wide beam was all the extra space. It meant you could have more rooms. Or, as he had chosen, *bigger* rooms and he loved the decadence of his spacious bathroom.

On autopilot he went through the now almost second-nature process of taking off his prosthesis and placing it outside the glass area. Still on autopilot he reached for the gleaming metallic railing that was attached to the tiles at waist height the entire way. He barely registered the gritty, high-grip tiles beneath his foot.

He flicked the taps and the water rained down on him nice and hot within seconds. He shut his eyes, forcing himself to relax. To clear his head of his sister's unhelpful suggestions. And Ava's unhelpful seduction.

And the unhelpful build of sexual frustration.

Just because he was horny didn't mean he should act on it. *Not with her anyway.*

He turned, letting the water sluice over his neck, flopping his head first forward then back, enjoying the heat on traps he'd had no idea were so tense. His eyes fluttered open. And that was when he saw it.

A lacy black thong hanging over the shower screen.

Pink ribbon weaved along the waistband and a little pink bow sat dead centre, another diamanté winking down at him.

She'd been wearing that get up under her clothes all day? His traps tensed again.

Crap.

Blake woke the next morning after another fitful sleep to dreadful off-key singing and the smell of frying bacon. His stomach growled and his mouth watered despite the assault to his ears.

He hadn't been sure what to expect this morning after their...disagreement last night and he'd lain awake wondering what kind of a post-spat personality she was.

Was she a flouncer, a sulker, a brooder?

It certainly didn't sound as if she was any of the above if her peppy singing was anything to go by. He reached for his leg and put it on, then reached for his T-shirt and pulled it down over his head. He'd taken it off during the night as replays of Ava straddling him had made the warm night quite a few degrees hotter.

He rubbed a hand through his hair, taking a moment before standing and facing her. Ava's singing stopped momentarily and he could hear the lower murmur of a breakfast news programme on the television. Blake hoped that Ken had some *news* for them this morning. Like they'd found the person or persons responsible for shooting up Ava's house.

She started *singing* again and he made his way to the kitchen and just stood and watched her for a moment as she boogied in front of the cooktop. The gown from last night was on again but was floating loosely by her sides and he felt a sudden kick in his groin at the thought that she might just be naked under there and if she turned around then—

She turned around.

Everything leapt to attention for a brief second and

not even the evidence of his own eyes—that she was indeed wearing something under that gown—could stop the rapid swelling of his erection. Because a spaghetti-strapped, clingy, not-quite-meeting-in-the-middle vest top and matching boy-leg undies on a tall, bronzed supermodel was something to behold.

Her face lit up. 'Ah.' She smiled at him. 'You're up. I'm making bacon butties.'

Blake swallowed. Up? *In more ways than one.* Was there anything more sexy than a woman in skimpy lingerie? Except maybe for a woman in skimpy lingerie cooking bacon?

Ava smiled as Blake's gaze roved all over her. *Yeh, buddy, this is what you're missing out on.* 'How'd you'd sleep last night?' she enquired sweetly.

Blake's eyes narrowed at the suspiciously smug question. So this was the kind of post-spat personality she was—a fighter.

Who liked to play dirty.

Well, he wasn't one of her entourage of men who fluttered around her and kissed her butt. 'Like a log,' he said.

Wrong choice of words as her gaze dropped to the area between his hips with its suspicious bulge.

Which *did not* help the suspicious bulge.

But then her smile slipped a little and a tiny frown knitted her brows together. He looked down at what she'd found so disagreeable and realised, unlike every other time she'd seen him, his prosthesis was on full display.

He supposed a woman as physically perfect as Ava would find his leg rather confronting. He felt absurdly like covering it up. And then he felt really freaking cranky.

Blake's teeth ached from clenching his jaw hard as he waited for her to say something. Something trite or clueless, something about how at least he still had one leg or how *marvellous* prosthetics were these days.

Instead she just dragged her gaze back up to look into his eyes. 'Take a seat. Eggs are just about done.'

CHAPTER EIGHT

THERE WAS NO news from Ken, although Ava Kelly was still the talk of the tabloids and breakfast shows. Speculation as to where she'd disappeared was rife and one talk-back radio station had even offered money to anyone who could produce pictorial evidence of her whereabouts.

Ken was far from impressed with that.

Blake was downright annoyed. He suggested Ava put Reggie to good use and sue their arses off for endangerment. She'd just shrugged, clearly so desensitised to press intrusion that the invasion of her human rights didn't even register.

They got under way again as soon as breakfast was done. They were travelling along a stretch of the tidal Thames and they had to fit into lock times that were mandated by the tide. His plan was to moor somewhere around Windsor overnight then on to Reading the next day where the Kennet and Avon canal began. Once they'd turned into it, they could putt along more lazily, but for now it was full steam ahead.

Or as full steam as possible when the speed limit was four miles per hour!

And Ava Kelly was your very distracting travelling companion.

Blake didn't think she was being deliberately distracting. She was fully bagged up again. Baggy shorts and shirt, her hair all tucked up in a cap, sunglasses firmly in place. She looked as anonymous as the next woman riding the canals.

But he knew what she had on under all those layers.

And that was pretty much all he could think about—every time she moved or talked or offered him something to eat. *Like freaking Eve with the apple.* In fact, even when she wasn't anywhere near him, he was thinking about her and what she might be wearing against her skin.

Did she have on the same spaghetti-strapped vest and matching boy-legs that had been under her gown this morning—the ones that displayed the most perfect belly-button probably ever created? Or had she changed into some other frothy, lacy, silky, maybe be-ribboned scraps of fabric when she'd changed into her outside clothes?

It was annoying how much brain space the speculation was taking up. He should be enjoying the gorgeous sunshine on his face, the breeze in his hair, the spectacular beauty of the English countryside. And while Ava had raved over the magnificence of Hampton Court, he'd barely registered it.

It wasn't good for his mood or his sanity, and it was the last straw when he caught himself trying to look down her top from his vantage point standing at the helm as she asked him a question from the bottom of the three stairs that led to the back of the boat.

'What?' he asked, when he realised he hadn't heard a word she'd said because he swore he caught a glimpse of red satin.

Ava, who'd deliberately leaned forward a little, gave him an innocent smile. 'I said are you ready for some lunch now?'

'Yep. But not here.'

Blake knew he had to get off the boat. Get away from the lure of her and red satin. Put himself amongst people, where he had to behave rationally. *And not tear her clothes off with his teeth.*

'There's a pub just up ahead,' he said. 'About five minutes away. We'll moor and eat there.'

'Fab,' she said and smiled up at him.

Blake pushed the boat a little harder.

Ava was enjoying watching the array of boats go by and
the sun on her face as they sat in the reasonably full beer
garden that fronted the river. They were sitting at one end
of a bench—the other end a family group were chatting
away oblivious to who was sharing their table with them.

By tacit agreement, Blake had gone inside and ordered
for them while Ava stayed out. Being incognito worked best
when she exposed herself to scrutiny as little as possible.
Sitting in a riverside beer garden just like any ordinary girl
was clearly possible, but the more people she spoke to, the
more she risked exposure.

She was pleased when Blake came back with two pints
of cold beer. It was warm in the sunshine and she felt hot
in her baggy attire. What she wouldn't give to be in her
bikini now, or at least in clothes that didn't cover her from
neck to knee.

'You remembered,' she said, smiling at him as she lifted
her glass and tapped it against the rim of his larger one.
'Cheers.'

Blake watched her guzzle it like a pro then lick the froth
from her mouth. *Sexiest thing he'd ever seen.*

'Mmm,' she murmured after taking several deep swallows, quenching the thirst the hot sun had roused. 'That
hit the spot. It's warm, isn't it?'

Ava put the beer down and pulled on the neckline of
her shirt, fanning it back and forth rapidly to try and cool
the sweat she could feel forming between her breasts. She
hadn't done it to provoke Blake but it was pleasing when
his eyes narrowed and followed the movement.

She was glad his sunglasses didn't obscure his eyes as
hers did. She liked knowing exactly where he was looking.

He looked kind of hot and bothered himself and she smiled. 'Aren't you roasting in those jeans?' she asked.

Blake shrugged. 'I'm okay.'

Ava regarded him. Did he always cover up his prosthesis? She'd been surprised when she'd seen it this morning. Not because she thought it was grotesque but because Blake always seemed so sure of himself, so confident, so…able. Seeing his leg had been a reminder that he wasn't, or at least that it wasn't so effortless for him.

'Do you never wear shorts?' she asked.

He dropped his gaze to his beer and took another sip and she could tell he was uncomfortable with the subject.

'Perfect weather for them,' she pushed as he turned his head to take in the activity on the busy river. 'You don't like people knowing?' Ava guessed tentatively.

Blake sighed as he turned back to face her, putting his beer down. 'I don't care who knows or doesn't know. Jeans…avoid conversations I *don't* want to have.'

Ava got the message loud and clear. But she wanted to have the conversation anyway. 'Like how it happened?'

'Yes.'

'What a hero you must be?' she guessed again.

Blake rolled his eyes. 'Yes.'

'How brave you are?'

He nodded. 'Yes.'

The level of chatter around them was sufficiently high that they could talk without fear of being overheard and Ava really wanted to know more about the circumstances of his amputation. The man had pushed her to the ground as someone shot up her house, purely out of instincts that had obviously been honed during his time in war zones.

As far as she was concerned he *was* a hero.

'How *did* it happen?'

Blake didn't really fancy talking about it with her, but at least talking was keeping his mind off her red bra. In fact maybe he could use it to his advantage. 'If I tell you, will you promise to not hang your underwear in my shower?'

Ava was momentarily surprised by his blatant blackmail. But it was satisfying to know that her *under*wear was getting *under* his skin. 'Deal.'

Blake took another sip of his beer. 'It happened the usual way,' he said dismissively. 'On patrol in the middle of nowhere. A roadside bomb. An IED. All over red rover.'

Ava should have expected the abridged version. 'Did anyone die?'

Blake steeled himself not to flinch at the question. 'Yes. One.'

Ava nodded slowly at another abridged version that told her nothing of the emotional carnage he must have borne. 'And the leg? Did you lose it straight away or after?'

'It was pretty mangled. They amputated it as soon as I hit the hospital.'

His words were flat, his answers matter-of-fact but Ava could see the tension in his muscle, the tightness of his jaw.

'That must have been…incredibly painful,' she murmured.

Blake gripped his glass as the sounds of his screams flashbacked to fill his head all over again. He wondered if people—if Ava—would think him so heroic if they knew how loudly he'd screamed. Lying in agony in the dirt, his eardrums blown out, the warm ooze of his own blood welling over the hand he'd reached down to try and stop the pain.

If they knew his brother-in-law lay dead beside him and Blake hadn't even given him a single thought.

'It was.'

Ava was about to say more. To push more. To ask more. But the waiter arrived, placing their ploughman's lunches in front of them and an extra bowl of hot chips for Ava, and Blake's white-knuckled grip on his glass eased as he picked up his knife and fork.

'Let's eat,' he said.

Ava sighed. *Conversation over.*

They didn't talk much over lunch, for which Blake was grateful. Ava seemed happy enough to drop her line of questioning and just eat and enjoy the sunshine, with occasional questions about their route for the afternoon.

He didn't really talk about what had happened to him—not with civilians anyway. His family knew the most of it. The army shrink knew more. Joanna at one stage had wanted to know every detail and had wanted to go over and over it ad nauseam and, even though it had been horrible and he'd dreaded seeing her number flash on his phone screen or hearing her wobbly, strung-out voice in his ear, he'd done it because he'd owed her.

The only people he could really talk to about it with any level of comfort were the guys he'd served with because they were the only ones who could *truly* understand any of it. But he rarely saw any of them and when he did, contrary to popular perception, none of them were particularly keen to rehash old war stories.

Talking about it with Ava wasn't his definition of fun but at least he'd won a concession from her so maybe it had been worth it.

He watched her as she laid her cutlery on her empty plate then reached for the tomato sauce bottle and squirted great dollops all over her hot chips, then sprinkled a heart-attack quota of salt over the top. She picked one up in her fingers, and ate with gusto, sighing a little sigh. She added two more to her mouth, then, before they were fully swallowed, another two.

A dollop of sauce smeared at the corner of her mouth and Blake's gaze was drawn to it—he couldn't help himself.

'What?' she asked around her mouthful of hot chips. Then she picked up the remnant of her beer and washed them down, licking her lips free of sauce and beer residue.

The woman made the simple act of eating into a sexual enterprise.

'Isn't your body supposed to be a temple or something?' he asked. 'Aren't supermodels supposed to always be on some kind of diet that involves no carbs and lots of egg-white omelettes and running on a treadmill for six hours a day?'

'Ugh, no thanks.' Ava shuddered as she picked up another chip and popped it in her mouth. 'My mother used to be strict about that stuff as I was growing up and—'

Ava stopped. She didn't want to think about her pageant-queen mother. It was a long time ago and it always put her in a bad mood and the sunshine and company were just too good.

'Anyway…I do exercise…mostly…but…' She sighed. 'I have to admit, I'm not a fan and it's hard to see the point when I'm one of those people who have good genetics with a great metabolism and can pretty much eat whatever without putting on weight. I've been really blessed like that.' She grimaced. 'I'm one of those women other women hate.'

Blake could see that. Most women he knew had some kind of body hang-up or other trying to keep up with impossible images in women's magazines. Images that she perpetrated.

'The thing is,' she said as she chomped on another chip, 'I just freaking love food. I don't know if that's because of Dad's influence or not but it's just…I don't know, like… air to me. I *need* it.'

'And,' she said, picking up another two chips and dipping them in a puddle of sauce on the bottom of the bowl, 'I'm starving all the time, which is why I cook a lot at home and wanted an amazing kitchen, which you—' she jabbed another chip in his general direction before popping it in her mouth '—gave me in spades. No pics of me at restaurants stuffing a three-course meal down then asking for seconds of dessert. I eat like a supermodel when I'm in public and then come home and cook up something amazing in my beautiful kitchen because by then I'm so freaking hungry I'm almost faint with it.'

Blake knew it shouldn't, but her appreciation of both his kitchen and for food in general turned him on. Just talking about how much she loved food had clearly got her all enthused and excited. She was using the chips to emphasise her points and her cheeks were all flushed and her freckles were standing out. He wanted to whisk her glasses off and see if the yellow highlights in her eyes were glittering fit to match the sun on the Thames.

There was nothing haughty or spoiled about *this* Ava, who was chowing down on hot chips and cold beer.

Ava chose another chip, realising there were only five left and she hadn't offered him any. 'Oh, God, sorry,' she said, picking up the bowl and pushing it towards him. 'Do you want any? They were so good I got carried away.'

Blake chuckled at her half-hearted offer. He couldn't see her eyes but he'd have been deaf not to have heard the reluctance in her voice. 'They're all yours,' he said, waving them back.

'Good answer.' She grinned as she dived for the remaining chips.

Blake's breath caught in his lungs. If *this* Ava straddled him right now his powers of resistance would be totally useless.

By six o'clock that evening they'd moored just upstream from Windsor Castle. The unparalleled views of the extensive grounds surrounding the castle as they had floated past had been amazing and Ava, who had apparently *met* the queen, had been excited to see the royal standard flying high from the round tower indicating Her Majesty was in residence.

After last night, Blake hadn't expected to enjoy the day as much as he had. He'd expected Ava to be petulant and

difficult—like a spoiled child who hadn't got her way—
but she'd been perfectly well behaved and he was smiling
to himself as he came in from outside, pulling a beer bottle
from the fridge and cracking the lid.

If Ava could keep up her ordinary-girl act and give the
sex-kitten/prima-donna a rest, it could be an enjoyable time,
while it lasted. Of course, it could be even more enjoyable
if he allowed himself to be seduced. But he was determined to show her he was one of the good guys. That she
could trust him.

A cutting board with chopped tomatoes and onions sat
waiting on the kitchen bench and fresh basil spiced the air.
Ava wasn't dancing around his kitchen and, as he'd heard
the pump kick in while he'd been checking the ropes, he
assumed she was showering.

His brain wandered to that delightful prospect before
he pulled himself back from the image. *Do not think about
her showering.* What he needed to do was go and grab
some supplies out of his room while she wasn't in it. Some
clothes and toiletries etc.

Except when he stepped into his bedroom he discovered
she wasn't in the shower. He pulled up short just inside the
doorway as his gaze fell on bare golden shoulders.

Ava looked up as Blake entered the room. Their eyes
met and there was a world of surprise in those few seconds. But there were other things as well, especially when
his gaze dropped and lingered at the point where her damp
hair brushed her collarbones.

There was a hell of a lot of want in that lingering contact.

They'd had a good time today. Blake had seemed to relax
more as the day had worn on and she was even left with
the impression that he might actually *like* her. Certainly
not how she'd felt after last night's debacle.

And there'd been something so sexy about the way he
handled the boat. Maybe it was the whole *Captain Capa-*

ble thing he had going on or maybe it was just the way his T-shirt had fitted snugly across solid biceps.

Either way, his attraction had cranked up several notches since last night and her belly tightened at the thought of just how capable he might be on the big beautiful bed right in front of her.

'Hi,' she said, breaking the silence that stretched between them.

'Oh, sorry,' Blake said, dragging his eyes back to hers—no easy feat considering she was dressed in nothing but a towel. 'I thought you were still in the shower.'

Ava shrugged and watched as his gaze followed the motion. She raised her hand to where the towel was firmly tucked into itself between her breasts and was satisfied when his gaze took the trip with her.

'Nope. Not any more,' she murmured. 'All fresh and clean.'

Blake took an absent sip of his beer that he'd forgotten he was even carrying. 'Yes.'

A small smile played on Ava's lips at his obvious distraction. Blake could deny himself as much as he liked in the name of honour but it was pretty obvious what he really wanted. 'Did you want something?' she asked. 'Or were you secretly hoping to catch me getting dressed?'

Blake frowned as the words yanked him out of his stupor. He really hoped she didn't seriously think he'd come into the room to cop a perve. He wasn't some horny bloke who let the content of his underpants dictate his actions. He'd proved himself to be pretty honourable under circumstances where most men would have cracked and she could take a flying leap into the canal if she thought otherwise.

But then he noticed that predatory gleam from last night in her eyes again, which suited all her languid feline grace, and he knew what this was.

Goodbye, ordinary girl. Hello, sex kitten.

Ava watched Blake transition from annoyed to wary

but she wasn't about to let it stop her. 'It's okay, you know, to admit there's something between us, Blake,' she said, gliding forward. 'To want to do something about it. I know that you feel you're in a position of trust but I'm not going to think any less of you.'

Even in a towel, with acres of tanned, toned flesh on display, she still pulled off a superior look better than anyone he knew. Maybe he should have let her off at the castle for the night with the Queen.

At least she wouldn't be here, naked but for a towel, tempting him to forget what was right, forget that every instinct he possessed warned him to stay way away from her.

Her shoulders were, oh, so bare, oh, so lovely as she pulled up in front of him. Right in front of him. He doubted he'd even have to extend his arm its full length to brush fingers along her collarbones. To yank her body flush with his.

Blake pulled his gaze up, meeting her frank, knowing eyes. A whole world of temptation stared back at him. 'Yes, but *I'll* think less of me,' he said.

She looked at him through half-closed lashes like some silver-screen goddess, one of her snooty little half-smiles playing on her mouth. 'I promise you won't have to *think* at all.'

She seemed to have shifted tack from last night—from brash self-assurance to coquettish flirtation and Blake decided he liked this Ava better. Almost as much as he liked the possibility of a little mindless sex despite the faint echo of warning bells clanging somewhere. He'd spent a lot of the last few years inside his head, thinking. Just like now. Letting that all go while he lost himself in Ava for a while was an attractive proposition.

He looked at her mouth, which was dead ahead. Right there, ready to claim, her lips two perfect arcs aside from the tiny dip in the middle of the top one that was incredibly fascinating. He'd really like to lick her just there.

And along those lovely collarbones.

It would be so easy. He leaned his shoulder into the door frame. 'Just leave my brain on the table by the bed, huh?'

Ava, encouraged by the way he appeared to be considering her words instead of rejecting them outright, broadened her smile. 'Well not entirely. Don't forget what they say about the body's largest sexual organ being the brain.'

Blake gave a soft snort. 'Only men with small penises say that.'

Ava was momentarily surprised by his quick, disdainful comeback and then she laughed. He was so serious and yet the quip had been fast and witty. If he'd just put a smile on that marvellous mouth it could even be classed as banter.

It definitely made him seem more approachable and her hopes soared. 'Well, that…' she let her gaze travel down to the area between his hips, then back up again '…counts you out.'

Blake's groin leapt to life at her blatant reminder. He could still feel the warm clamp of her hand around him. How right it had felt when she'd stroked him last night good and firm, *just the way he liked it.*

His fingers itched to touch her. To stroke along her shoulders, up her throat, along her mouth. But being dressed in only a towel was a double-edged sword. Sure, she might look sexy and gorgeous and utterly accessible, but it also reminded him of how vulnerable she was and he was reminded of her pallor and fright straight after the shooting.

He was reminded that she was under his protection. 'I was never in,' he said and hoped it sounded definite.

Ava sensed he was wavering. She smiled at him, not convinced that *he* was convinced. Still *convinced* she could talk him round if she trod carefully. God knew, her abdominals were scrunched so tight in anticipation she'd never need do another sit-up again.

She sighed as she took a half-step closer. 'You're hard on a girl's ego, Blake Walker.'

Blake didn't trust her easy-going reply, not when she

was somehow closer than she'd been a moment ago. Some-how more enticing.

Okay, this was getting dangerous. *Time to step away from the sex kitten.*

He took a mental pace backwards. 'I'm sure your ego can take it,' he said dryly.

Ava sensed his withdrawal but tried not to panic. She could still reel him in; she was sure of it. 'You know us su-permodels.' She shrugged again for good effect, satisfied when his gaze locked on her shoulders. 'Always needing someone around assuring us we're beautiful.'

Blake battled the urge to assure Ava with his tongue down her throat, or in her ear or licking all the way down her body. Instead, he straightened in the doorway. 'Oh, you're beautiful, Ava Kelly,' he said. 'But I'm going to take a shower.'

A cold one.

Ava raised an eyebrow. 'Is that an invitation?'

Blake's groin roused further as a bunch of possibilities played through his head. *A very cold one.* 'No. It is not,' he said, then turned away.

No, no, no. Ava knew she'd lost him. Stubborn man. But she refused to give up. 'Blake.' She slipped a hand on his retreating shoulder.

Blake tensed. He wished she wouldn't touch him. He didn't want her to touch him. It made him want to touch her right back. And a bunch of other things too. He turned.

'What?' he asked impatiently. 'Time to offer me some more money?'

Ava gasped as if he had slapped her. It stung that he was throwing her bribery back in her face. But most of all it stung because he made it sound so cheap.

'Go to hell,' she snapped. 'You think you're such a goody bloody two shoes? You think self-denial is so freaking honourable? Go right on ahead, you believe it, whatever helps you get through the night, *buddy.* But you and I *both*

know how badly you want this, how much you want to succumb and how it's only a matter of time before you give
into temptation.'

Blake was taken aback by the ferocious yellow glitter
in her eyes as all Ava's fierce feline juju leapt out at him.
She was pretty angry at him and yes, he conceded, maybe
that *had* been a low blow.

But she was hitting pretty low too and her accuracy
was startling. Still, no way was he going to let her know
that. 'Ava, I wouldn't succumb to temptation if you were
lying naked on my bed,' he said, jabbing a finger towards
it, 'with beer poured all over you.'

Ava knew there were only two possible comebacks to
that. One was to slam the door in his face. Choosing the
other, she reached over and plucked the beer out of his
hands. 'Wanna bet?'

CHAPTER NINE

ANY ISSUES AVA might have once had with taking her clothes off in front of strangers had died very quickly when she'd hit the big time. Over a decade in front of one camera or another she could very definitely look at her body with objectivity—the way the people who paid her did. For them she was just a canvas for an artist aka fashion designer to decorate in whatever way he/she wanted.

Years on catwalks where quick crowded changes were paramount and modesty something that nobody worried about had taught her that nudity was passé and certainly nothing to be ashamed of or worried about. Parading around in clothes that often left little to the imagination—be it on the catwalk, or for a magazine shoot or a television commercial—had compounded this view.

So lying on her back on Blake's bed, wriggling to the very centre, then peeling her towel away was no biggie for her. Even if he'd never seen her in a single magazine, he'd been given a pretty good preview last night.

Except, at the last moment, as the towel fell away, she raised the leg closest to him, bending it at the knee and placing the foot flat on the bedspread, shielding the full view of her lower half from his eyes, providing a modicum of decency. She wasn't sure why she did it but she felt suddenly reluctant to strip off all the way.

Aware Blake was watching every single move, she raised

herself up on one elbow and, facing the ceiling, she tipped her head back, her hair brushing the coverlet, and took a long deep swallow of his beer. Then she held it just above the hollow at the base of her throat.

Blake could *not* tear his eyes away from a butt-naked Ava sprawled in the middle of his bed. An erection big enough to cause cerebral infarction from lack of blood flow to his brain pressed painfully against the zip of his jeans.

Her breasts were firm, the slight side swell utterly tempting, her nipples enticingly lickable. Her belly dipped down from her ribs and the play of muscles there as she held her torso semi-upright was fascinating, drawing his attention to the inward swirl of her perfect belly button.

He swallowed. 'Ava.'

She looked at him for long moments, her gaze knowing, and he wished he could turn away from the delectable sight of her, but he was powerless to resist. She gave him a slow sexy smile as if she knew he was waiting for the show, then she slowly tipped the bottle up.

Blake felt her gasp hit him square in the groin as cold beer spilled down her naked skin. He watched as it flowed down her sternum, branching out as it ran down her body, sending rivulets across the swell of her breasts, her nipples ruching at the contact of the cold liquid. It dipped into the valleys of her ribs and washed down the centre of her abs, spilling down her sides and pooling in her belly button.

Her leg hid how much lower it might have flowed, which was just as well. He did not want to think about *that* combination of beer and woman.

It wasn't conducive to clear thinking.

He shut his eyes, thinking about all the reasons why this was a bad idea. Damsel in distress. Knight in shining armour. Protector. Defender.

Honour.

Trust.

He opened his eyes in time to see her collapsing back

against the bed. She held her hand out to him and said, 'Please,' like freaking Eve lying down on a bed of apples. *Really red, really juicy apples.*

And something snapped inside him then. There was only so much provocation he could stand and what the hell he was holding out for when she was a grown woman who clearly knew her own mind was a mystery not even he could fathom any more.

He strode into the room until he was standing beside the bed, looking directly down at her. *At all of her.* Every last inch. A beautiful contradiction in femininity. Smooth and firm. Soft and supple—interesting curves and sculpted muscles.

And very, very sticky.

His gaze tracked the path of the beer from her throat to where it had pooled in her belly button and then lower. Yes, it had run lower, drenching the trimmed strip of hair at the apex of her thighs.

And he was suddenly very, very thirsty!

Her foot dangling over the edge of the mattress rubbed against his leg and streaked heat up his thigh, urging him on. And he wanted to. A part of him wanted to join her on the bed immediately and lick every last trace of sticky, beery residue off her until she was begging him to stop.

And then do it all again.

She lay looking up at him with lust in her eyes and a knowing little smile, as if she'd ghost-written the Kama Sutra, but part of him could see past her brash outer confidence now to the vulnerable woman beneath, and that was who he wanted to touch.

Ava suppressed the growing need to squirm under his scrutiny. Her nipples got harder. Her breath grew shorter as his gaze lowered and lingered between her legs, streaking heat *everywhere*. She could feel the trickle of moisture where he stared and she wasn't entirely sure it was all beer.

His gaze pulled away again and fanned up and over

her. He was looking at her as if he wanted to eat her up but wasn't sure where to start. Other men looked at her as if she had a staple through her navel. As if she were some prize they'd won.

As if they'd scored with a supermodel and they were looking at her to perform like one.

Blake was looking as if he was trying to map her entire body. Locate all her hotspots. Work out what he was going to do to them. And how long he was going to spend doing it.

Like a recon mission.

Like a soldier.

Either that or he was committing her to memory before he did a bolt. Something she doubted she'd survive now he'd brought her right to the brink of arousal. *Without so much as touching her!* Because she was very, very aroused.

'Blake?'

Her voice was husky and she dragged in some quick breaths to dispel the annoying weakness. But she was pleased when it seemed to bring him out of his intense study.

Not that he answered her or even said a word. He just locked gazes, put a knee on the bed beside her leg, leaned onto his hands and lowered himself slowly down, his head level with her belly. When he was a whisper away from the puddle of beer in her belly button, he broke eye contact and touched his mouth to her abdomen, his tongue swiping at the now warm liquid.

Ava gasped, her back arching, her hand reaching down, ploughing through Blake's dirty-blond hair. She held him against her, afraid he was going to stop or that she was going to float right off the bed.

Don't stop, she wanted to say, but there was no need as the hot flat of his tongue swiped and swiped in ever-widening circles around and around her belly until she was whimpering and calling his name.

'Blake.'

Blake looked up from his ministrations—all the way up. Over her belly and up her ribs, skimming her breasts, fanning up her throat to her mouth, opening and shutting, silently begging him for more. 'Yes?'

She raised her head and looked at him with eyes that weren't quite focused. 'I...I...'

I...what? *What?* Ava couldn't speak. All the man had done was lick her belly—after making her wait for two days *and several minutes*—and she was putty in his hands. But it didn't matter because he was lifting his head, travelling up, up, up and before she could protest the lack of him down there he was up top, his mouth on hers, his hands in her hair, his body pressing her into the mattress.

And he felt so good all she could do was hold onto him and follow where he led.

And he led with spectacular commitment. His mouth opening wide, demanding hers do the same, kissing and licking and sucking, dragging every morsel of lust and need and want from her lips. Groaning against her mouth, absorbing the husky timbre of her noises that alternated from strong and strident to weak and whimpery and desperate. Joining the shuddery husk of his breath with hers.

And all the time his hands stroked and caressed, from her neck down, flowing everywhere, whispering heat and seduction wherever they touched. Promising lust and good times and secrets she never knew existed.

Eventually, the drugging lash of his mouth left hers and she protested. 'No, no,' she moaned, grabbing for him, reaching for his head, for his face, to bring him back where she needed him, to her mouth, where he'd poured all the lust and desire she'd never have known was even there but for this bubble of time.

But then he was kissing her again, saying, 'Shh, shh,' against her mouth, hushing her with his kisses and the magic of his hands as they stroked over her belly. And then, pushing her arms up above her head, restraining her there saying, 'I want to lick beer off you,' as he licked lower, down her jaw, her neck, her chest.

And it might have been weak of her but Ava, under the influence of his very clever tongue, let him.

Blake knew the moment she let go. The moment she stopped wanting it to be about them and let him make it all about her. It was the second his mouth opened over her nipple and, even though every muscle in her body tensed, her back arching up, pushing more of the gloriously hard tip against his palate, she clearly surrendered to him.

Her hands stopped questing, stopped pushing against the bond of his, trying to move, trying to reach for him. Her body melted into the mattress. Her head fell back, her mouth open wide as if breathing was all she could manage.

He liked that.

He liked that he'd made her incapable of anything but the very basics of life.

It allowed him free rein and he took it mercilessly, tasting her everywhere. Ravaging her nipples to hard peaks over and over until she begged him for release. Leaving there to head south, laving her belly with his tongue again, skating around the juncture of her thighs despite the desperate lifting of her hips, using his tongue to devastating effect on the sensitive skin of her inner thigh, her legs wide open, the intoxicating mix of beer and woman ratcheting up his heart rate, making his mouth water.

Making him want to bury his head there and taunt her with his tongue until she came long and hard. But he was determined to have all of her as he licked down to her bikini-red toenails.

Ava was lost in a world where she floated somewhere off the ground in a place full of sensations that swirled and skipped in a kaleidoscope of pleasure, drenching her in sweet, sticky rain. And she surrendered to it—lolled in it. Twirling and sliding, getting absolutely soaking wet.

There was something missing; she knew that. It nagged

at the back of her mind but she couldn't quite pinpoint it. Then his fingers brushed up her thighs then teased against the core of her and she cried out at the intensity of it, wanting it to end, urging him to get her there.

But knowing somewhere inside her she *never* wanted it to end.

His fingers stroked and swirled, round and round, going hard, then backing off, going hard again until she was begging him to end it. But he didn't. Instead the hard probe of one finger slipping inside her had her crying out, then another as his wicked tongue laved the flesh of her inner thighs.

And just when she thought she couldn't take any more his mouth was on her, tasting her, his tongue circling hard around the sensitive bud, and she bucked against him, crying out.

That was what was missing. She wanted to taste him too. Wanted to put him in her mouth and know the contours of him.

The velvet and the steel, the sweet and the salt of him.

She didn't want to just lie here and be serviced.

'Blake…' she panted trying to sit up, trying to reach him. 'Blake…please…let me taste you too…'

'No,' came the muffled reply, his hand clamping down hard on her abdomen, the vibrations of his voice exquisite torture against her ravaged flesh. 'You. Just you.'

Ava fell back against the bed. She should have said no. *No, no no.* Insisted they be equal partners in this. She should have been worried that his honourable streak was going to see her fulfilled while leaving him wanting but she'd just used up her one last rational thought.

So she surrendered to him and this time he didn't back off with fingers or tongue, he just drove her higher and higher until Ava could feel herself drawing tight, so tight she didn't think she'd be able to breathe, and for a moment as everything coalesced into one powerful pinpoint of time her lungs seized and she swore for a second or two she did actually stop breathing altogether.

Then air came rushing into her lungs and she grabbed it, sucking in and out as ecstasy slammed into her. She grabbed Blake's head, holding him where he was as it undulated through her body, bowing her back off the bed, forcing a primal cry from the deepest part of her soul.

And she rode it all the way to the end.

Blake's heart rate was still unsteady as he lazily kissed and sucked his way back up Ava's body. She was still away in the land of sexual limbo and he was taking full advantage of her inebriated state to touch her some more, to make sure he'd lapped up every last trace of beer from her very delectable body.

He hadn't known what to expect from this—sex with Ava. Frankly he'd spent most of his time trying *not* to think about it. But he'd never thought it would be so fulfilling just to get her off. For someone as sexually confident as Ava she'd given him control so easily—as if her control freak was a mask she wore but was only too happy to lose. And her complete immersion in what was happening to her body had been heady stuff.

He swirled a nipple in his mouth and she moaned long and low as he felt it grow hard against his tongue.

He released his mouthful to look up at her. 'You're back,' he murmured.

Ava smiled at him. She twined her fingers in his hair, as best as she was able amidst the short strands 'Barely. I think I died for a short while.'

Blake chuckled, stroking his fingers up her arm. 'It's okay. I would have given you the kiss of life.'

Ava rolled her eyes. 'That's what got me into this mess.'

Blake raised an eyebrow as he stroked lazy fingers over the rise of her right breast. 'Would we call this a mess?' Of course the situation had mess written all over it but enjoying Ava's body had been divine.

Ava shut her eyes as the caress hummed right through her still-buzzing middle. 'No,' she said, opening her eyes. 'We would not.'

Blake dropped a kiss on her shoulder and nuzzled her there. 'Good.'

Ava stroked his hair, her mouth brushing against the ends, absently noticing the way it just brushed his nape, falling far short of the neckline of his shirt.

'You still have all your clothes on,' she said.

Blake lifted his head. 'What can I say? You were insatiable.'

'I think we need to do something about that, don't you?' she asked, reaching down to the small of his back, and grabbing a handful of his shirt.

Blake considered her for a moment. He wanted to get naked and do the wild thing with her. God knew his erection was still a living, breathing mammoth inside his underwear and he wanted to feel it buried deep inside her. But it wasn't simply a matter of just taking his clothes off.

'Duck,' she said to him as she ruched his shirt up his back, pulling it up to his shoulders. 'I want to even the playing field.'

Blake looked down at her body, his gaze lingering in all the places he'd been. 'I like uneven playing fields.'

Ava rolled her eyes. 'I bet you do.' She tugged on his shirt again but he resisted. 'Blake?'

Blake sighed. 'There's not exactly a sexy way to remove a prosthetic leg,' he said.

Ava blinked. She'd forgotten about his leg. Hadn't thought about the…logistics of sex with a prosthesis. Or how it made Blake feel. 'Does it…embarrass you…to take it off in front of someone…in front of a woman?'

'No,' he said. Not that he'd ever taken it off in front of a woman who personified human beauty. 'But it's a bit like stopping to put a condom on…it's a big dose of reality, which can be a bit of a passion killer.'

Ava regarded him for a moment or two. 'Well, we can't have that, can we?' she murmured.

Then she pushed against his shoulders and, as he fell back on the bed, she followed him over, rolling up until she was straddling his hips. The juncture of her thighs aligned perfectly with the bulge in his jeans and she pressed herself against him, revelling in the hard ridge. It was satisfying to hear the suck of his breath and watch his eyes shut as his big hands came up to bracket her hips.

'Feels like the passion's very much alive to me,' she murmured.

Blake opened his eyes. She was a sight to behold. Her drying caramel hair fell in fluffy waves against lovely shoulders thrust proudly back. It emphasised the firmness of her high breasts boasting erect, perfectly centred nipples. Her stomach muscles undulated and her belly button winked as her hips rocked back and forth along the length of him.

Each pass rippled urgent pleasure through the deep muscle fibres of his belly. It also caused a fascinating little jiggle through her breasts and Blake couldn't drag his eyes off them.

'I don't know,' he muttered. 'I think I've died and gone to heaven.' Then he curled up and claimed a nipple.

Ava gasped as Blake's hot mouth sucked her deep inside. She raked her fingers into his hair, capturing his head to her chest, and holding him fast. His teeth grazed the tip and her head dropped back. He switched sides, grazing the other nipple as he sucked it hard and deep, and when his fingers toyed with the other one her lips parted on a moan as she dragged in much-needed air.

Blake revelled in the moan. But he wanted more. He wanted to taste her. To swallow her moan as it vibrated against his tongue. He broke away, sought her mouth, found it as she protested his absence.

'Shh,' he said against her mouth, his hands stroking down her naked back. 'I've got you.' And when she moaned again and opened wide to the invasion of his tongue he kissed her deep and wet.

Released from the intimate torture of her nipples, Ava was able to think a little clearer—even though all he'd done was switch from one form of havoc to another. The man could kiss for England! But she needed more than that now. He was thick and hard between her thighs and *that* was what she needed.

Ava grabbed for his shirt and pulled it up his back. Then she broke off the kiss and hauled it the rest of the way off, tossing it behind her. And then her hands were on his smooth, naked shoulders and she sighed and pressed a kiss to them, they felt so good.

His hands slid to her breasts and she shut her eyes for a moment as his thumbs stroked across her nipples and he started kissing her neck.

Then she shoved his chest hard and watched him fall back against the mattress. 'Hey,' he protested, reaching out for her.

But she just shook her head and said, 'My turn.'

And if Blake thought she looked amazing before it was nothing to how she was looking now, astride him buck naked staring down at him as if he were the main course and she were *starving.*

Ava gazed down at all his broad magnificence. The dusting of hair over his meaty pecs, the solid firmness of his abdominals. A work-honed chest. A *real* man's chest. She stroked a finger right down the centre, from the hollow at the base of his throat to where the waistband of his jeans stopped her journey. Muscles contracted beneath her finger and his breathing became more ragged.

And then she just had to taste him.

Blake groaned as her mouth tentatively touched the spot where her finger had started its journey. Her hair fell forward, brushing his chest, and he slid his hand to her shoulder and stroked down her back, revelling in the feel of her skin beneath his palm as he revelled in the feel of his skin beneath her tongue.

By the time she got to his nipples there was nothing tentative about her touch. They circled and circled as he had done to her. Sucking and licking. Flicking her tongue back and forth over them and he shut his eyes and let the sensations wash over him.

Then she headed lower. Exploring his ribs, his stomach, his belly button.

And then lower.

His zip came down, his underwear was peeled back and at the first touch of her tongue to his screamingly taut erection he bucked and cried out. And then she was relentless. Swiping her tongue up and down the length of him, filling her hot, hot mouth with him, sucking him in deep and hard, feeling so good, so right.

He buried one hand in her hair and the other one in the coverlet, gripping the sheets as she drove him out of his mind.

It wasn't long before the tug of an orgasm made its presence known. Under her ministrations it was inevitable that he would build quickly but he didn't want it to be like this.

Not the first time.

'Ava,' he said on an outward breath. 'Stop.' She didn't stop. If anything she sucked harder. 'Ava,' he said again, curling half up, pulling at her shoulder, pulling her up.

'Wha...?' she asked, looking at him, a frown on her face.

Blake almost gave in. Her mouth was moist and swollen and she had a glazed look in her eyes that almost undid him.

'If you don't stop that now it's going to be all over and I want to be inside you when I come,' he said.

Ava's brain took a second to power up again but quickly

got up to speed. She smiled at him. She'd been wondering what it would feel like to have him hot and hard inside her for the last few months. 'Condoms?'

Blake smiled back and nodded towards the bedside table. 'In the drawer.'

She was off the bed and back at his side again in fifteen seconds, tearing at the condom with shaking fingers. And then she was sheathing him, and then straddling him and leaning over him, easing herself into position, kissing him as she slowly aligned herself.

He gripped her hips hard as she slid home and her gasp and his groan mingled as they both just stilled for a moment and enjoyed the feel of their joining. And then she was pushing up and away from him, sitting proudly, her breasts bouncing as her hips undulated, finding a perfect rhythm.

Her hair was wild, and her yellow-green eyes were even wilder, all feline and primal. And she didn't look haughty now, riding atop him. Actually, no, she did. She looked like a madam on her steed and he bucked hard into her as she picked up the pace.

'God, you're magnificent,' he groaned, holding out his hands to her.

'You're pretty magnificent yourself,' she gasped as she intertwined her fingers with his.

And then neither of them talked. They just moved. Up and down. In and out. Harder. Faster. Building, building, building. Using their joined hands to lever their actions, pushing hard against each other's palms, finding every inch and every bit of depth they could.

And then she was gasping, her eyes opening wide, and she was crying out, 'Blake! Blake!' and the urgency of it all slammed into his belly and he felt himself coming apart too, joining her, calling out her name too, 'Ava!' as he came and came and came, his heart rate off the scale, bucking and thrusting like a machine, determined to give her every last bit of him, their hips slamming together as he drove and drove and drove up into her.

And he didn't stop, not even after they were both spent, not until she collapsed on top of him.

CHAPTER TEN

IT WAS AFTER eight the next morning when Blake finally stirred. He'd always been an early riser but, given that he and Ava had spent a lot of the night burning up the sheets, it was hardly surprising that he'd slept in.

She felt good spooned against his chest. As did his erection, cushioned against the cheeks of her bottom, and the handful of her hip beneath his palm. He stroked his hand down her thigh and was rewarded with an enticing little wiggle.

'Morning,' he murmured as he nuzzled her neck.

Ava smiled sleepily as the prickles of Blake's whiskers beaded her nipples. She deliberately pressed her bottom back into him as she stretched. 'What time is it?'

Blake shut his eyes as her moving weakened his resolve to get going. 'Time to get up.' They should have been under way by now.

'Really?' she asked, slipping her hand behind her and between their bodies, finding him big and hard and ready. And not for a day on the water. 'I think,' she said, giving him a squeeze and smiling when he sucked in a breath, 'you're already there.'

Blake kept his eyes shut as her hand moved up and down the length of him. 'I am,' he said, his own hand dipping down her belly and disappearing between her legs.

Ava gasped as his fingers brushed against the thoroughly abused nub, already begging for more. She let him go, slipping her arm up behind his neck, anchoring herself as she angled her hips to accommodate the slide of his erection between her thighs and the glide and rub of it along the seam of her sex.

'Man-oh-man,' she moaned. 'That feels so good.'

Blake, getting under way completely forgotten, whispered, 'You ain't seen nothing yet,' in her ear and proceeded to rub and glide from one side while his fingers worked her from the other and it wasn't until she was begging him for completion that he whispered, 'Condom.'

And Ava didn't need to be told twice.

A couple of hours later they stirred again. Blake dropped a kiss on her neck. 'We really do have to get going at some stage today,' he murmured.

Ava's eyes fluttered open. 'Why?' she asked as she turned in his arms, one arm sliding over his waist, her head resting against the soft pillow of a pectoral muscle.

Blake propped his chin on top of her head. 'Because I'm on a schedule, here. I can't stay on holiday for ever.'

Ava smiled. 'You're a schedule kind of a guy, aren't you?'

He nodded. 'And proud of it. That's what over a decade in the military does for you. That's what got you your reno on time,' Blake reminded her. He looked down at her head. 'I've seen those behind-the-scenes-at-a-fashion-show docos on the telly—those things run to tight schedules too.'

'They do,' Ava conceded. 'And I can run to a schedule as professionally as the next model. But when I'm on *holiday...*' she glanced up at him '...schedules go out the window. That's *the point* of a holiday. It's all about being flexible.'

Blake smiled down at her. 'Oh, you're *very* flexible.'

Ava rolled her eyes. 'Why can men never resist an opening?' But she kissed him anyway because he was right there and he looked even more tempting this morning than he had last night.

'My point is,' she said, pulling back from the kiss, 'you're on holiday. You don't really have to *do* anything or *be* anywhere. For instance, we could stay here in bed all day together. We could kiss and cuddle, have lots more sex, doze off, wake up, watch some telly, eat gourmet snacks I can prepare. You know…just have some fun?'

Blake felt the usual clench of his gut at the word *fun*. He knew it shouldn't affect him, that he had as much right to a full happy life, *to fun*, as the next person, but it still felt wrong to be enjoying himself when so many guys he knew couldn't.

'We can do whatever we want,' Ava continued, oblivious to Blake's consternation, 'because *we're on holiday*.'

Blake forced himself to smile and push the downer thoughts away. *He was allowed to have fun.* His shrink had told him that over and over.

'Ah, but *you're* not on holiday,' he reminded her, injecting a deliberately teasing tone into his voice. 'You've just hijacked mine. *Bribed* your way in if my memory serves me correctly.'

The thought was sobering but Ava refused to let it get her down. 'Well, it feels like it. I haven't had a lot of idle days since turning fourteen.'

Blake heard the pensive note in her voice and stroked his finger down her face. The last thing he wanted was to drag her down too. 'Okay, then, you win. A rest day.'

Ava laughed. 'In that case I better get us something to eat. Cos I don't think either of us are going to be getting much rest.'

Blake smiled. 'No,' he said. 'Allow me.'

Ava quirked an eyebrow. 'You? You can cook? You who only had a six-pack of beer in the fridge two days ago?'

'I can manage coffee, toast and fruit,' he said indignantly as he rolled onto his back, then swung into a sitting position and flicked the wall-mounted telly on with the remote, handing it to her. 'See what the media is saying about your situation and then check in with Ken.' He reached for his leg propped against the wall. 'I'll get us some breakfast or brunch or lunch…or whatever it is.'

He went through the motions of getting into his prosthesis as Ava flicked through the news channels. He could have had crutches just to get around the boat, a lot of amputees used them for domestic purposes, but he hadn't wanted to become reliant on them, preferring to always use his leg.

Blake looked around for his clothes but as he had no idea where they'd ended up last night he figured he might as well just throw on some new ones.

Ava's gaze was drawn to him as he skirted around the bed, briefly interrupting her view of the telly as he strode to his wardrobe. His brawny masculinity wasn't diminished by the prosthesis, if anything it emphasised it—a silent testament to his heroism. But there was just something kind of surreal about it and she couldn't help but laugh.

He turned and quirked an eyebrow at her and she clamped a hand over her mouth. *Way to be sensitive, Ava.* 'I'm sorry,' she said, embarrassed by her behaviour. 'I'm not…I don't—'

'What's the matter?' he interrupted and she could see the teasing light in his indigo eyes. 'Never seen a naked man with a fake leg?'

'You look like Bionic Man,' she blurted out, still clearly suffering from foot in mouth. But he did. His broad chest and shoulders and his narrow hips were perfectly proportioned. The hard, powerful quads and calves of his good leg balanced out the hard moulded plastic and titanium lines of the prosthetic. He looked half man, half machine.

Strong. Super strong.

Ava kicked the sheets off and swung her legs over the side of the bed. 'It's kind of a turn-on actually.'

He watched her walk towards, him, one hundred per

cent naked, one hundred per cent up to no good, staring at his body as if she wanted to eat him. His groin fired to life.

'You're not going to be one of those chicks who has a thing for amputees, are you? Hangs out on all the forums and dating sites?'

Ava shook her head as she sank to her haunches in front of him. 'No,' she said, looking up at him, past the rapid thickening happening before her eyes. 'Just for you.'

Blake's heartbeat pounded through his ears as her gaze feasted on the jut of his now fully fledged erection. 'Ava,' he warned as the muscle fibres in his belly and his buttocks turned to liquid. 'Food...Ken...'

'Later,' she dismissed as she raised herself up, her hands gliding up his legs and anchoring at the backs of his thighs, her mouth opening around him.

Blake's groan came from somewhere primitive inside him as hot, wet, delicious suction scrambled his brain of any rational thought. He reached for the cupboard and held on for dear life.

Later that afternoon, Blake was sitting propped against the headboard of his sleigh bed, idly flicking through channels as Ava dozed by his side. It was another warm day and they'd kicked off the sheets a long time ago so she was lying on her back stark naked, completely comfortable with her nudity.

His phone vibrated on the bedside table and he checked it. Charlie. *Still hanging with the supermodel?*

Blake smiled. *Yes.*

The reply was fast. *Slept with her yet?*

Blake's gaze wandered to her naked body, his chest filling with something akin to contentment. His fingers slid across the touchpad. *You are a pervert.*

Another fast reply. *So that's a yes?*

Blake gave a soft snort as he typed his reply. *Goodbye.*

A little yellow face with a dripping tongue hanging out

its mouth appeared on the screen and Blake shook his head at his brother's juvenile wit as he returned the phone to the bedside table.

He flicked his gaze back to the telly just as an ad break came on. He was about to change the channel when Ava came on the screen. 'Hey,' he said, giving her a gentle nudge. 'Wake up, you're on the telly.'

He couldn't believe he was in bed with a woman whose face was on the telly. Her celebrity had been easier to wrap his head around when he'd just been the guy renovating her house.

Ava stirred, opening her eyes to see the cologne commercial she'd shot last year. 'Oh, yeah.' She smiled, half sitting, wriggling back, insinuating herself between Blake's thighs, snuggling her bottom in and draping her back to his stomach, her head under his chin. His arms encircled her waist and they watched it together.

Ava was proud of the commercial and had had a lot of fun filming it with one of England's most dashing young actors. It was moody, edgy, very dark and sexy, suiting the bouquet of the cologne.

Blake wasn't so enamoured as Ava, showing almost as much flesh as she was now beneath a transparent white hooded gown, was chased and then caught, her dress ripped open down the front and her neck *and parts distinctly lower* thoroughly ravaged by a dark, brooding, shirtless man.

The voice-over said, 'Beast. For the animal in us all.'

Okay, no actual prohibited-for-PG-viewing bits could be seen, but it was a very fine line and the subliminal messages were heavily sexual.

'What do you think?' she asked, turning her neck to look at him as the commercial ended.

Blake cast around for something to say that wouldn't annoy her when clearly she was pleased with the results. 'I think if I owned these,' he said, his hands sliding up her belly to her breasts, 'I wouldn't want anyone else touching them.'

Ava smiled. She wasn't surprised by his reaction. People outside the industry didn't understand how it worked. She glanced back at the telly. '*I* own these,' she said, sliding her hands up under his, cupping her own breasts, his hands falling away.

She looked down at herself, at her hands, aware he was looking too before letting go.

'Anyway…it's all just make-believe. We did that shot about a hundred times, there's a full set of people watching you, a director telling you a bit to the right, a bit to the left, hot lights, make-up people, a ticking clock. It's not as sexy as it looks.'

'So how do your boyfriends cope with that? Because, frankly, I'd want to punch that guy in the head.'

Ava laughed. 'Well, that's very Neanderthal of you.' She knew she shouldn't find that attractive but somehow it fitted with his whole ex-soldier, Bionic Man persona and she was secretly thrilled.

Blake guessed he should apologise for his prehistoric possessive streak but he didn't. 'I just don't get how it works.'

'Which is precisely why I don't have *boyfriends*. Lovers, yes, boyfriends, no. Lovers are disposable, boyfriends tend to get jealous. And only from within the circles I move in because you have to be in the biz to understand how very little all that—' she waved her hands at the screen '—means. Models, actors…they know how it works.'

'Wow,' he said derisively. 'You really are slumming it with me.'

She glanced up at him but he was smiling down at her and didn't seem to be too insulted. She ran her hand down his thigh. 'I'm making a special exception for you.'

'So, you don't have…relationships?' Didn't all women crave relationships? Connections?

Hell, didn't all human beings?

Ava looked down, following her hand as it absently caressed his thigh. 'No. Best not to. Relationships require trust. I've had some major disappointments in that sector earlier in my career, a couple of guys talking to the press and with Mum and Paul…let's just say I wised up pretty quickly.'

'That sounds kind of lonely though…'

Okay, he wasn't exactly King of relationships either, but not because he didn't believe in them. He just wasn't sure if damaged goods made very good partners.

Ava traced the outline of Blake's quad with her index finger as she shrugged. 'I don't have time for men who want to hold me down…hold me back. I don't have time for their petty jealousies. I have a finite amount of years I can do what I do and I'll worry about relationships after. For now dating and the occasional spot of casual sex with a guy in a similar situation to me suits just fine.'

Blake absently rubbed his chin against the fineness of her hair as he absorbed her very definitive views.

Ava turned her neck to face him, unnerved by his silence. She'd come to her relationship conclusions a long time ago the hard way and it had never mattered to her before what anyone thought.

But somehow it did right now.

'You think that makes me cold and unfeeling?'

'No,' Blake said and meant it.

Ava had to be the least cold and unfeeling person he knew. Sure, her snooty *touch-me-not* public image was meant to convey that, but if he'd learned anything about her at all these past three days it was that she was a strange mix of hot and cold. Strong and vulnerable. Public and private.

And he felt privileged to know the real woman beneath the distant haughty smile.

'I think you've taken control of your life and you know what you want. A lot of people never do that.'

'Damn right,' she said as she looked back at her hand on his thigh, his chuckle vibrating against her back. 'What about you and relationships?' she asked. 'You're still single.'

Ava stopped tracing the quad on his good leg and drew a line with her finger down the thigh of his amputated leg, which seemed almost the same length as its opposite number. The quad almost as meaty. 'Has this stopped you?'

Blake looked down at her hand. 'No. But there's a lot of…baggage attached to me…and I'm not much of a talker. So…that makes it hard to see past the outside to what's underneath.'

Except Ava had. Ava had known him for three months before she'd even been aware he *had* a prosthesis. She hadn't treated him differently—no pity for the cripple or reverence for the returned war hero. She'd been demanding and snooty and utterly self-absorbed. As testy with him as everyone else around her.

And despite what a pain in the butt she'd been, he suddenly realised how refreshing it had been. How deep down he'd looked forward to going to her place for a slice of equity in a world where everyone in his orbit treated him just a little bit differently than they had before he'd lost his leg. He knew they didn't mean to or even realise that they were, but he was sensitive to the subtleties.

Would Ava have been so demanding and critical if she'd known he was an amputee? Or would she have *made allowances*?

'Yep,' Ava said. 'I hear ya.' She totally understood where he was coming from with that—people never looked past her outside package.

Her palm skated to the end of his thigh and tentatively cupped his stump. His quad tensed and for a moment she thought he was going to pull it away. But he slowly relaxed into her hand and she became aware of its rounded contours.

It felt so…smooth. So…healed. So…innocuous.

Nothing liked the jagged, shredded mess it must have been to have lost it. She shut her eyes against a hundred television images she'd seen over the last decade. She couldn't even begin to imagine what he'd been through. The trauma. The pain. The loss.

'Does it hurt?' she asked after a moment.

Her hand felt cool against the stump and so pretty against the blunt ugliness of it, it took all Blake's will power not to pull away. 'No.'

'Did it?' she asked. 'Sorry, of course it did… It's just that I saw this documentary once, interviewing returned soldiers, and there was this one guy who'd lost a leg and he said he was in so much shock at the time he didn't feel anything, no pain…nothing. He didn't even realise his leg had been blown off until he woke up in hospital. He doesn't have any memory of losing it at all.'

Blake's screams, never far away, echoed in his head. Unfortunately for him, his memory had perfect recall. 'It hurt,' he said grimly. 'A lot. I screamed like a baby.'

Ava turned at the blatant contempt in his voice. 'Your leg was blown off,' she said, frowning at him. 'That must have been *incredibly* painful… I can't even begin to imagine…did you think you didn't have the right to express that pain?' She lifted her hand off his leg to his face. 'Do you think *anyone's* going to judge you for that?'

Blake saw compassion and pity in her eyes. Just as he'd seen in countless people over the last three years. And, thanks to his shrink, he'd learned that it was a natural human reaction to a sad and shocking situation. But he still had problems accepting it at face value because the truth was he judged himself more harshly than anyone else could have.

'There were other men injured in the blast, Ava. Men who were *my* responsibility.'

Ava didn't need to be a psychiatrist to tell Blake was

judging himself plenty. 'Blake…are you telling me you still have to be a leader when you're bleeding in the dirt somewhere with a severed leg?'

He stared at her. 'They were my men. They looked to me.'

Ava's skin broke out in goose bumps at the utter desolation in his voice and the bleakness in his eyes. 'Even when you're injured?' she asked gently. 'Wasn't there some kind of second in command?'

Blake nodded. 'Yes. He was dead.' Colin, dead in the dirt beside him.

Ava shut her eyes. *Not helping, Ava.* 'I'm sorry,' she said, twisting in his arms, moving, straddling him, settling her butt on the tops of his thighs until they were face to face. 'I'm so sorry,' she repeated.

Then she lowered her head and kissed him—slow and sweet. 'So sorry,' she whispered against his mouth as she pulled away, hugging him close.

It felt good to have his arms circle her body, bringing her in closer until they were flush, his head nestled against her neck, her chin on top of his head.

'What was his name? Was he married?'

Blake shut his eyes, dragging in big lungfuls of her sweet-smelling skin, trying to block out the image. 'Colin,' he said. 'And yes, he was married.'

Ava could hear the roughness in his voice and she held him closer for long moments. 'Do you blame yourself?' She pulled back to look at him. 'For him dying?'

Blake looked up into her earnest gaze. That wasn't an easy question to answer. There was the logical answer. And the emotional one. And they both blurred into each other.

Ava didn't wait for him to reply. 'Would *he* blame you? This…Colin?'

Blake shook his head. It was a complicated situation but he didn't have to think about it to know the answer to that one. 'No.'

'Well, isn't that your answer?' she asked.

Blake shook his head. *If only it were that simple.* '*I* was supposed to look out for him,' he said.

'Because he was one of your men?'

Blake shook his head. 'No. Well...yes, but...' Blake paused, the desire for her to understand pushing hard at his chest. 'Because he was one of my closest friends and... my brother-in-law.' He placed his forehead against her collarbone, his lips brushing her chest. 'Colin was Joanna's husband.'

Ava shut her eyes as his heavy words felt oppressive against her chest. The guilt in his voice was undeniable. Oh, *dear God*—how had Blake survived that? She tightened her arms around him.

'I'm *so* sorry,' she said.

Having to face his amputated leg every day must be a constant physical reminder of what he'd lost. Having to face Joanna, *his sister,* must be a constant *emotional* reminder. She was surprised he'd ever got his life together again.

That must have taken real strength.

Her breath stirred the hair at his temple and Blake held her tighter too. He was used to superficial sympathy from people but with Ava wrapped around him like this it felt real.

'Have you talked to anybody about any of this?' she asked after a few moments.

Blake gave a soft snort, pulling back from her neck. 'Ad nauseam,' he said. 'The army supplies a shrink.'

'So they should,' she muttered. 'Has he helped?'

'*She,*' Blake supplied and smiled to try and soften the topic and erase the anguish from her gaze. 'And yes, actually. I was kind of resistant but, yeh...I'm in a much better place after talking to her than I had been.'

'Well, that's...good,' Ava said, feeling slightly mollified.

Blake smiled and made a concerted effort to drag himself out of the funk they'd descended into. Even he knew this was a far cry from the *fun* she'd prescribed earlier.

'It is,' he murmured, dropping a kiss on the fluttering pulse at the base of her throat. 'Although I prefer other forms of therapy.'

Ava shut her eyes as his tongue traced wet circles up the hard ridge of her throat, sinking into the heat and the thrill of it. 'Like what?'

Blake smiled as her reply buzzed against his lips and she dropped her head back to give him better access.

She might not be able to do anything about the demons in his head or erase all the bad stuff that had happened to him, but she could definitely give him her body. Maybe that was wrong, maybe she should be trying to get him to talk and open up, but she couldn't help but think that a man who'd been through what Blake had been through deserved to choose his own path to wellness.

And right now, in this moment, there was something she *could* do to help him forget for a little while.

She was definitely up for a little sexual healing.

CHAPTER ELEVEN

THE NEXT THREE days drifted by in a perfect little bubble. A bubble where she wasn't a supermodel and he wasn't a one-legged pleb totally out of her league. No lady and the carpenter thing. Just good company and great food and amazing weather.

Laughter and sunshine.

Long days of lazily navigating the waterways of southern England. Waving to fellow boaters. Operating locks. Eating at pubs.

And the nights? Long, hot, sweaty nights of a more frantic persuasion. Eager to be naked and explore. Being bold and forthright. Pushing each other to the limits of their sexuality.

Never quite getting enough.

It was as if they both knew deep down it could never last and therefore the everyday masks they wore to face the world were stripped away. Pretence was shed and there was only room for the real and the raw.

The investigation was progressing according to Ken. They were tracking down leads, leaving no stone unturned. But no arrests had been made and his advice to keep lying low remained the same.

Ava should have been getting antsy. Ordinarily she would have been going out of her mind, not doing anything, worrying about her time out of the limelight and how that might impact her career. Reggie certainly was. Fretting about it day and night with his increasingly desperate calls and texts. Pleading with her to allow him to feed the press something…anything…any morsel to keep them fed and watered and interested.

But after a decade of unfettered availability, anonymity was seductive. A simple life on the water with a simple man was even more seductive.

And while the British press and the paparazzi were in a feeding frenzy over *Ava Watch,* obsessing over her whereabouts, reporting any faux sighting as if she were Elvis, Ava was revelling in her new-found freedom to just…be.

To not put on make-up.

To not go to the gym every day.

To stuff her face with banoffee pie at a pub and not have to watch for a telephoto lens.

To kiss Blake publicly and not worry that she was going to read about her engagement or possible pregnancy in some tabloid the next day.

But the bubble burst late on day six with a very sombre intrusion. And it was the beginning of the end.

Blake's phone rang while they were having dinner at a pub in Devizes. They were talking about the Caen Hill staircase lock they were going to tackle the next day. A good six hours of lock after lock, twenty-nine in total.

Ava watched him frown at his screen and push the answer button. He didn't say much, just, 'Right…right,' and 'When?' and 'Where?' but his face got grimmer and grimmer and she could feel a cold hand slowly closing around her heart.

'What's wrong?' she asked as he pushed the end button.

'Change of plans. I have to go to a funeral tomorrow.'

Ava blinked. No more information appeared to be forthcoming. 'Oh. Okay…who?'

'A guy I served with.'

His reply was clipped and his face, which had been

animated about the adventure ahead just a few minutes ago, was suddenly as bleak and forbidding as a thunderclap. 'Where?'

'A little village outside Salisbury. I'll hire a car in the morning. I can be back by nightfall.'

Ava nodded. She wasn't sure what she should do, or say. Should she push him for more—did he want that? Or should she take him back to the boat and distract him? She looked down at their half-eaten meal, suddenly not remotely hungry. She looked around at the cheery pub crowd enjoying the late evening warmth in the beer garden.

'You want to go back to the boat?'

Blake nodded. 'Yup.'

They walked along the towpath in silence. Blake was tight-lipped and she didn't even attempt to hold his hand as she had on their way to the pub. Once they were inside the boat and Blake had locked the door behind them she turned to him and said, 'Do you want to talk about it?'

Blake shook his head, grabbing her arm and yanking her flush with his body. 'No,' he said and slammed his mouth down onto hers as he swept her off her feet and carried her into the bedroom.

Distraction it was.

The next morning dawned cool and miserable. They woke to rain patting lightly on the roof and a grey light barely making it through the curtains.

The symbolism was not lost on Ava.

'I can come with you,' she said, snuggling her back into his front, her bottom into his groin, reaching for the bone-deep warmth that seemed to have evaporated in the cold grey light.

She felt him tense and hastened to assure him. 'Not to the funeral,' she clarified. 'But for the trip. For…company.'

She expected him to say no. And for a long time he didn't say anything at all, his warm hand firm and unmoving on her belly. 'Sure,' he said. 'Company would be… good.'

And then he was kissing her neck and his hand was sliding between her legs and Ava opened to him, welcoming another session of feverish sex, knowing instinctively that Blake needed a physical outlet for the grief he couldn't express any other way.

A few hours later they'd been driving for an hour in virtual silence when Ava couldn't bear it any more. The landscape was as bleak as the mood in the car and her indecision was driving her nuts.

Say something, don't say something.

But in the end, she couldn't pretend they were just going for a Sunday drive in the countryside.

'What's his name?' she asked.

Blake's knuckles tightened on the steering wheel. 'Isaac Wipani.'

Ava frowned. 'That's an unusual surname.'

'He's a Kiwi. His father was a Maori. Died when he was a boy.'

'Didn't you say you served with him?'

Blake nodded. 'He joined us from the New Zealand Defence Force after he met and married an English girl.'

'How old was he?'

'Twenty-nine.'

Ava almost asked him how it happened. But really, did it matter? A man was dead. A young man. A soldier. 'Did they have children?'

'Two.'

If anything, Blake's face got grimmer and any other questions died on her lips. She wished they had the kind of relationship where she could slip her hand onto his thigh, to loan him some comfort. She knew they'd shared something special the last few days but what were four days and nights of sex compared to a lost comrade?

And he looked so incredibly unreachable in his dark suit and even darker mood she was too paralysed to try.

They made it just in time for the funeral. Blake deposited her in a pub opposite the churchyard where the service was taking place and she sat at a cosy booth cradling a coffee, looking out of the rain-spattered window at the bleak day.

Lucky for her, Joanna had thought to include clothes for when the Indian summer came to an abrupt end, which it was always bound to. The black jeans and duffel coat were baggy but the tie at the waist helped and a slouchy knitted beanie even looked quite funky and fashionable when she tucked her hair up inside it and let it pouch to one side like a beret.

It was too dark inside to wear her sunglasses but Ava still felt utterly incognito.

Half an hour later and on to her second coffee, Ava noticed movement across the road and watched as six uniformed soldiers hefted a coffin draped with the Union Jack high on their shoulders through the churchyard towards the headstones. A woman in black and two little children holding her hand came next. Then other people, silent mourners, followed at a respectable distance. A lot in uniform. A lot of civilians too.

Ava could see what was happening very clearly from her seat as the procession stopped at a clearing on the outer edge of the headstones, fresh earth piled nearby. She knew she shouldn't watch. That it was a private affair, not some spectacle to gawk at. But the sight of those two little kids broke her heart. Her breath was heavy in her lungs and she couldn't seem to look away.

Her eyes sought Blake through the crowd. Needing to find him, to see him, to know he was okay. She started to panic when she couldn't locate him, her eyes darting around more desperately. And suddenly he was there—one grim-faced man amongst a group of grim-faced men, mainly uniformed standing to one side—and she breathed again.

A loud cry cracked the laden air like a whip and Ava startled at the unexpectedness. It had come from the direction of the gravesite and her eyes scanned for the source.

It was a man's cry. A warrior's cry. A call to arms. It had easily penetrated the four-hundred-year-old stone walls of the pub and no doubt was even now echoing right down the high street if the heads poking out of windows were any indication.

She looked back towards the church in time to see movement down the far end of the gathering, about a dozen khaki-uniformed men, in two lines, one behind the other.

The men were bouncing on the balls of their feet, their knees slightly bent, their arms folded out in front of them. They advanced towards the coffin sitting at the end of the waiting hole in the ground, calling out and grunting, their faces fierce. Then it became more organised, with the men all chanting in unison, stamping their feet in time as they slowly closed in on the coffin, slapping their hands against their chests.

Ava recognised it as the special dance she'd seen the New Zealand rugby team do at the World Cup a few years back. As the men surrounded the coffin, their forceful rhythmic chants echoing through the entire village, she felt tears well in her eyes and goose bumps prick at her skin.

It was raw and primitive and so achingly mournful she couldn't remember ever seeing anything so…savage be so utterly beautiful.

As suddenly as it started, it stopped, the angry chants falling silent, and there were long moments where nothing but the light patter of rain could be heard. Then, one by one the group of soldiers straightened, tall and strong, and slowly walked backwards from where they'd come, their solemn gazes locked on the coffin, their moving tribute to a brother-in-arms complete.

'Such a shame, isn't it?'

Ava dragged her gaze away from the window at the sudden intrusion. She looked up to find the woman from behind the bar, who collected her empty coffee mug. She held out a box of tissues and Ava realised her face was wet.

'Thanks,' she said, taking a couple and dabbing at the tears.

'Such a lovely family. Jenny, the widow, she grew up just outside here, went to school just down the road,' the older woman continued as she wiped Ava's table down. 'They got married in that church.' She shook her head, tucking her dishcloth in her front apron pocket. 'Offered him a full military funeral, you know, but he never wanted that. He was coming home in three weeks…'

Ava nodded even though she didn't know. Didn't understand. Probably never would. All she could think about was Blake and what had happened to him. What if he'd died? What if she'd never known him?

The thought was so awful she could barely breathe.

'Another coffee, luv?'

She nodded. 'Yes, please.'

Ava had almost finished the third cup when the pub door opened, letting in a blast of cold, miserable air and a rowdy bunch of uniformed men and a smiling Blake. She waved at him as he looked around for her and he headed towards her.

'Hi,' Blake said as he reached the booth. He smiled at her and then frowned as she barely managed one in return. She looked as if she'd been crying. 'Are you okay?'

Ava shrugged. 'I saw that…dance.'

'Ah.' He nodded. 'The haka.'

'Yes, that's it.'

'It was a funeral haka,' he said. 'Some of the guys Isaac served with in New Zealand were over here.'

'It was…' Ava rubbed her hands up and down her arms. Even though the duffel coat was thick she still felt chilled.

'Blake, you dirty dog!'

Ava was kind of pleased for the booming interruption. She wasn't ready to articulate how deeply the funeral haka had affected her.

'You never told us you had a bird waiting for you,' a strapping great blond guy said, slapping Blake on the back. 'And a very nice-looking one at that. How are you, darlin'?' he said, holding out his hand, which Ava duly shook. 'I'm James but they just call me Jimbo.'

'Ava,' she said after a slight hesitation and a quick glance at Blake. It might not have been a common name but it was hardly unusual.

Jimbo certainly didn't bat an eyelid over it. 'Hey, guys,' he called over his shoulder. 'Come check out Blake's bird. Bring those beers over here and a champagne for the lady.'

'Sorry.' Blake grimaced. 'I hope you don't mind?'

Mind? Blake was actually smiling, which, considering his recent grimness, was a miracle. It was the most comfortable she'd seen him apart from when he was sanding wood or steering the boat.

Ava quirked an eyebrow at the man who had interrupted them. 'Make it a beer, Jimbo.'

'Oh, mate.' Jimbo laughed. 'You're on a winner there.'

Blake smiled down at her and said, 'Yeh. I think you're right,' and Ava smiled back, suddenly warm all over.

The next several hours, squashed into a booth with five strapping men, were the most educational of Ava's life. She'd have thought the mood would be sombre, and certainly there was talk about Isaac and toasts drunk to him, but mainly they just talked guy stuff and joked around with each other.

Ava was good at talking to men and fitted into the easy banter as if she'd been born to it. Jimbo, who was drinking steadily, would look at her every now and then with narrowed eyes then look at Blake and say, 'She looks really familiar.'

But she'd just shrug and tell him she had one of those faces and change the subject, getting him to tell her another story about what Blake was like during basic training, which Blake weathered like a trouper.

In fact all four of the guys who'd joined them seemed to have great stories about Blake and she encouraged them outrageously. Clearly he was well liked and respected and she was enjoying hearing about that part of his life—before he'd become so serious.

She also listened to Jimbo's female woes. The only single man at the table besides Blake, clearly he found women puzzling. She dished out some sensible advice about what women wanted and explained why infidelity was generally a deal breaker for women.

'You're lucky to have her.' Blake rolled his eyes as Jimbo repeated the decree for the tenth time.

'I don't know,' Ava said. 'Maybe I'm lucky to have him.'

'Oh, you are, you are,' Jimbo agreed. 'Good. Honourable. And brave. The man was awarded the second highest decoration for bravery you can get for what he did.'

Ava stilled. This from a man who had rejected the term hero over and over? 'What did you do?' she asked, turning to Blake.

Blake shook his head. 'It was nothing,' he dismissed. 'I was just in the right place at the right time.'

'Pulled a wounded soldier and four kids from a house fire while some bastards shot at him,' Jimbo supplied.

Ava stared at him as silence descended around the table. 'You did?'

Blake sighed. She was looking at him differently. He hated that. 'Anyone would have done it,' he said.

Jimbo burped loudly. 'Nah,' he said belligerently. 'I don't think I would have.'

A murmur of *me neither* rattled around the table and Ava

quirked an eyebrow at him. 'They're lying,' Blake said. He knew these guys inside out and back to front. 'Every one of them would have.'

'Yeh, but it was you,' Ava persisted. 'You who ran into a burning building, *under fire*, and pulled a wounded man and a bunch of kids out.'

'Because I was *there,*' Blake said, exasperation straining his voice. 'It's not like you think about it—you just react. I went in to get Pete and there were a bunch of kids in there too. What was I going to do, leave them?'

Ava shook her head. 'Of course not.' Blake would no sooner turn his back on them than he had on her in her hour of need. 'Sounds like hero material to me,' she said.

'Cheers to that,' Jimbo said, raising his glass, oblivious to the undercurrent between Blake and Ava. 'Captain Blake Walker, my hero.'

Blake opened his mouth to object. He wasn't going to have a bunch of guys still serving their country while he *sanded wood* toasting him as a hero.

'And Ava, his good looking bird. Never was there a man with such great taste in women.'

Blake didn't have a comeback for that. Neither did his good-looking bird. So they laughed along with the rest of the table until someone changed the subject.

'Stop looking at me like that.'

It was after five and they'd been driving for ten minutes. Blake could feel Ava's sideways glances like prickles beneath his ribs. He didn't want to have a conversation with her about the revelations of the day. It was bad enough she knew—he could do without the analysis.

Seeing the guys he'd served with again was always a bittersweet experience. But today had been a sombre day, a day where they'd laid a mate to rest. It wasn't the time or place to be talking about an event that happened eight years ago during his first tour of duty. Some ancient history *glory* that the brass had deemed worthy of recognition.

'So...you don't think you deserve the medal, is that it?'

Blake sighed. 'I don't think they should give out bravery medals for an act of common human decency. Servicemen do stuff like that every day in war zones,' he dismissed. 'I was just doing my job.'

Ava couldn't believe how blasé Blake was being. 'You saved the life of four kids and a soldier.'

'No, Ava, I didn't,' he said wearily. 'Pete died.'

A cold hand squeezed Ava's gut. 'He didn't make it?'

'No. He did not. Between the bullet to his gut and his burns, he passed away en route to hospital.'

Some of his bleakness leached across the space between them and settled over her like a heavy skin. How had that made Blake feel?

'I'm so sorry,' she murmured. 'That's...awful.'

'Yeh, well...that's war for you.'

Ava didn't know what to say to that. How could she even begin to imagine the things he must have seen? She looked out of the window at the grey day, misty rain forming streaky rivulets of water as it hit the glass. She'd been given a unique insight into him today, seeing him through the eyes of a group of men who clearly liked and respected him.

Ava wished she knew that man. Or had known him, anyway. She had a feeling he didn't exist any more.

Blake brooded for the next hour as they drove in silence. He hadn't meant to be so harsh with her, but he'd been to one too many funerals over the last decade and they had a tendency to mess with his head. Their closeness of the last few days seemed a distant memory now and he was sorry he'd been the one to destroy it, especially when all he really wanted was to get lost in her for a while and forget about the world and how insane it could be.

Her phone rang, the sound of rock music shattering

the oppressive silence. She pulled it out of her pocket and looked down at the screen before looking at him.

'It's Ken,' she said as she quickly answered it.

Blake assumed from the one-sided conversation and Ava's palpable relief that the police had finally caught the culprit, a fact she confirmed when she hung up a few minutes later.

'They made an arrest,' Ava said, smiling at him.

A heaviness descended upon Blake's chest. 'Who?'

'Grady Hamm.'

Blake frowned at the cartoonesque name. 'There's somebody in this world called Grady Hamm?'

Ava laughed. 'Yes. There is. He's an agent. Isobella Wentworth's agent.'

'Okay...and she is?'

Ava rolled her eyes at him. Hadn't everybody in the world heard about the seventeen-year-old catwalk débutante? 'An up-and-coming model. Britain's next big thing? And up for the same advertising campaign I am.'

'Ah.' The penny dropped. 'And he shot up your house to keep you out of the picture for a bit?'

She nodded. 'Well, he didn't shoot it up. He paid someone else to do it but, yes...it was just a scare tactic, apparently.'

A surge of anger jettisoned into Blake's system and he gripped the steering wheel as he remembered how frightened Ava had been. There was nothing *just* about it. 'A scare tactic that worked.'

'Yes. Until Isobella found out and dobbed him in.'

Blake whistled. 'That must have taken some balls for a teenage wannabe to turn in her agent.'

Ava nodded in agreement. It did. She knew the kind of fortitude that took intimately. 'I owe her, definitely.'

Blake contemplated the road for a few seconds as the full implications of the arrest sank in. 'So, you're free to go back home,' he said, injecting a cheeriness that felt one hundred per cent false after such a sombre day.

'Yes.' That should have been exciting but Ava felt as if they had unfinished business between them.

'It's time for your stitches to come out anyway,' he said, trying to be practical.

Ava looked down at the sticking plaster on her palm. 'Yes,' she said again.

'You should take the car as soon as we get back to the boat. You could be in London by nine.'

Ava knew that not only sounded feasible but sensible. But there was no way she was leaving Blake tonight.

Not after today.

'I'll go in the morning,' she said.

Blake opened his mouth to protest. There was no reason for her to stick around—their arrangement had only ever been temporary. But her phone rang again. 'Reggie.' She grimaced as she answered.

'Ava, darling, you have to get back here pronto!'

Reggie's voice was shouting in her ear as he spoke over what could only be a huge gaggle of press all yelling at him in the background. She could picture him now standing on the top of his steps leading into his Notting Hill office.

'Listen to them,' he said over the din. 'Come back, get a picture with Isobella. They're going nutso down here.'

Ava shook her head as she pulled the phone slightly away from her ear. She couldn't. And she couldn't explain why either. She just couldn't. 'I'll be back in the morning.'

'Ava…' Reggie spluttered. 'Don't be ridiculous. This is the kind of publicity you just can't buy.'

Ava was sure it was but that wasn't the point as she glanced at Blake. 'I'll see you tomorrow,' she said and hung up on his continuing protests.

'He's right, Ava.' Blake had heard every shouted word in the whisper-quiet confines of the hire car.

Ava shook her head. 'I'm not leaving tonight.'
'Ava.'
'I'm. Not. Leaving.'

CHAPTER TWELVE

AVA WASN'T SURE how long she'd been asleep when a loud cry woke her from her deep post-coital slumber. Her eyes flicked open and for a few seconds in the dark, her heartbeat thundering in her chest, she grappled to orientate herself. Then the cry came again—anguished, full of pain—and there was movement beside her and she realised Blake had vaulted upright in bed.

She groped through a groggy brain and leadened muscles to make sense of what was happening as he rocked back and forth.

'Blake?' She reached over and flicked on the lamp, her eyes shutting as the light hit them. 'What's wrong?' she asked, her hand sliding up his bare back as her eyes slowly adjusted to the light.

Blake sucked in a breath, biting back the expletive and another bellow of pain. 'It's my leg,' he seethed at the all too familiar sensation of hot jagged metal jabbing into his stump. Like the blast pain all over again. He raised his thigh and slammed it down against the mattress over and over trying to ease the crippling burn.

Ava shook her head as the mattress reverberated with the pounding. His leg? What did he mean? 'What's wrong with it?' she asked over his guttural groaning, looking down at it for signs of redness or bleeding or anything that could be causing him so much pain.

But it looked exactly the same as it always had.

He didn't answer her, just groaned louder as his movement grew more frantic and he became increasingly distressed. He kneaded his fisted hand so hard into his quad all the way down to his stump she winced and then he started pounding it, lifting his fist up then bringing it down hard.

'Don't, stop it,' she said, tears threatening in the face of his inconsolable pain and the brutality of his actions. She felt utterly useless. 'Please,' she said, pulling at his arm. 'Stop…you'll hurt yourself.'

He ignored her, shaking her hand off, his seething breath sucking noisily through clenched teeth as he pounded at his leg.

Ava didn't understand what was happening. Was he having a nightmare? Some kind of a flashback. Was he awake? 'Why are you doing that?' she asked, grabbing for his arm again.

'Because it helps with the phantom pains,' he yelled trying to shrug her restraining hands off.

Ava vaguely recalled having read an article on phantom limb pain a few years back. Something about residual nervous involvement in the amputated limb. Not that she remembered a single skerrick of anything that could be useful right now.

'That helps?' It was hard to believe anything so brutal could be used to treat pain—it seemed counter-intuitive.

'Yes.' Blake could already feel it starting to ease its grip. 'Pressure on the stump helps.'

Ava blinked. *There was pressure and there was pressure.* Surely it was going to be bruised tomorrow? Before she could think about it, she was shifting, moving, kneeling on her haunches between his legs. The fact that they were both naked hadn't even registered.

'Let me try,' she said, placing her hand over his fist, pushing it away, quickly replacing it with her hands, wrapping them around his stump and applying firm even pressure, squeezing rhythmically.

Blake felt himself slowly relax as Ava's hands worked their magic. He doubted they would have had any effect had it not already started to ease up—but they felt cool and heavenly now as the pain proper started to fade.

Ava concentrated on the job at hand, determined to at least try and help him, satisfied as he seemed to be slowly relaxing, his breathing settling, his death grip on the sheet with his other hand easing. 'Does this happen often?' she asked.

Blake shut his eyes and tried to focus on his breath and not the pain as the shrink had counselled. 'In the beginning quite a lot but I was one of the lucky ones able to get on top of it with medication…and time.'

Ava looked up at him. He had his eyes shut and despite his body slowly relaxing he looked haggard and tense in the lamplight. 'But it's obviously not cured.' She couldn't bear the thought of him, here alone, going through this with no one around to comfort him.

'I usually wear a sock-thing to bed over the stump, which is a good maintenance strategy that seems to keep them at bay. But…'

Blake opened his eyes to find her looking at him.

Ava didn't need him to finish. 'I've been here and you haven't been wearing anything to bed.' Guilt washed over her and tears pricked her eyes again—had *she* been responsible for this relapse?

He shrugged. 'It's okay. I doubt the funeral helped, either. I'm sure my shrink would say there's some psychological component as to why this is happening tonight.'

He sighed and rubbed a hand along the back of his neck, shutting his eyes again. 'It's been a hell of a day.'

Ava ducked her head as the tears threatened to become a reality. A hell of a day? It had been a hell of a *life* for him.

Serving his country. Earning a medal for bravery and

just brushing it off as if it were nothing because he truly believed he'd only done what any decent human being would have done. Paying bodily for that belief. Still paying. Still going to funerals. Still waking in the night to excruciating pain from a leg that was no longer there.

The stump was smooth beneath her hand now but the pain… She couldn't bear the thought of the pain he must have endured. If what she'd seen tonight was just a tiny indication of how it must have been in those moments straight after the explosion, she didn't know how he'd got through it.

The haka chants drummed through her head with each knead of her hands—the anger and the anguish washing over her, swelling in her chest, building and building, pressure in her throat and her lungs and pricking at her eyes and nose.

Blake felt something warm and wet on his thigh and looked down to find a single drop of moisture. He glanced up at Ava's downcast head. 'Hey,' he said, trying to look under her curtain of caramel hair.

He slid his hand to her jaw and gently lifted her chin to find tears dampening her cheeks. 'Why are you crying?'

Ava shook her head. She couldn't answer. She knew if she said one thing everything would come tumbling out and that would not be pretty because it churned in a big ugly mass inside her with no real cohesion.

'Ava. It's okay,' he murmured, smearing a newly fallen tear across her cheek with a thumb. 'I'm fine now. The pain's gone. You helped,' he assured her. 'You helped a lot.'

He dragged her closer and she shifted until she was straddling him, her arms around his neck. He looked up at her, kissing her nose and eyelids and her cheeks. Kissing the tears away. 'Shh,' he said. 'Shh.'

The lump in Ava's throat became bigger. She'd never met a man so…good. He reminded her of her father and she clung even harder to his neck

'Talk to me, Ava,' he murmured quietly as he dropped butterfly kisses all over her face. 'Talk to me.'

She shook her head. 'I can't...I can't bear the thought of the...pain you must have been through,' she said, trying to talk past the constriction in her throat. 'You've been through so...much and here's me with my own pathetic little troubles. For crying out loud, you have no leg, you have all this guilt about Colin and get...terrible pain and you have to keep going to funerals all the time and I...and I...'

'Oh, Ava, no...shh,' Blake said, pushing his hands into her hair, cupping her face so she was looking right at him. 'Someone shot at your house—'

Ava could feel more tears clogging in her throat and squeezing out of her eyes. 'But it was just to scare me. It wasn't for real...not like what you've faced.'

'Hey,' he said, pushing her hair back off her face. 'I was there. It was pretty real if you asked me.'

Ava nodded even as her brain dismissed the sentiment. There was real and there was *real*. 'Were you scared...over there?' she asked.

Blake nodded. 'Sometimes...yeh.'

A sob rose in Ava's throat. Blake who was strong and brave had felt fear and pain and been exposed to so much loss because his country had asked it of him. 'Why do we fight each other?' she whispered.

Blake felt helpless in the face of a question he had no clue how to answer. Her yellow-green eyes were two huge pools of compassion and anguish. 'I don't know,' he said.

And then he kissed her because that he did know. He did know how he could make it better. For tonight anyway.

The parting the next morning was a lot harder than Ava ever imagined it would be. They weren't *just* two people who had shared a boat for a week. He'd been more than the safe haven she'd asked of him. They'd shared a bed. Intimacies. They'd opened up their bodies and shared themselves.

More than either of them had ever shared before with someone other than their nearest and dearest.

It was another rainy day and Ava snuggled into her coat as they stood by the hire car saying their goodbyes. 'Maybe we could see each other…when you get back to London,' Ava suggested.

She'd never been with anyone like Blake—for good reason. But maybe it was time to revisit that?

Blake shook his head, remembering the constant presence of media in her life, the way the paps had bayed for a comment at the roped-off area the night of the shooting. And that commercial they'd watched together with the guy ripping off her gown and ravaging her.

He really didn't think he'd be very good with stuff like that.

'I think you and I live in very different worlds,' he said. 'I don't think I could live in yours and—' he glanced over at the boat '—I'm pretty sure you don't want to live in mine. Best to quit while we're ahead.'

Ava nodded. He was right, of course, but there was part of her that didn't want to let go.

'I'll see you around no doubt at the charity functions,' Blake added. 'The Christmas Eve fund-raiser is going to be huge. They've booked out the London Eye and I have a feeling Joanna's going to be working her new patron like a dog.'

Ava smiled. 'I look forward to it.'

Blake opened the door for her. 'Goodbye, Ava,' he said.

He could easily have leaned in and kissed her but, in his experience with Ava Kelly to date, he had trouble stopping at just one.

Ava nodded. 'Thank you for everything,' she murmured.

Blake grinned because the weather and the mood of the last twenty-four hours had been sombre enough without continuing it. 'It was my pleasure.'

She grinned back. 'And mine.'

And then she ducked into the car and he shut the door

after her and she started it up and within a minute she was watching him grow smaller and smaller in the rear-view mirror.

The bubble had well and truly burst.

And for two long months she didn't see him. The frenzy and the endless speculation about Ava and Isobella had died down thanks to an A-list celebrity cheating on his wife, and the whole tawdry affair blew over. Ava went to America for ten days, and scored the new commerical. She did the talk show circuit—now more in demand than ever—and she and Reggie made inroads on her calendar for the next year while cultivating new contacts.

She flew to Milan and then on to Paris. All the designers wanted her because of her rekindled buzz and Reggie made sure they paid. But when she strutted onto the catwalk and caused a mini-sensation thanks to her recent notoriety the cameras popped and people noticed what she was wearing.

September became October back in the UK and all trace of that blissful bubble of sunshine on the English canals had vanished. The weather was bleak and dreary. Cold with endless drizzle that seeped damp into everything including the marrow.

Ava thought about Blake constantly. Wondered what he was doing. Wondered how his holiday had gone. If he was back at work yet. She picked up the phone to call or text him a dozen times a day. But never followed through.

Which was just as well—she was too busy anyway. There weren't too many nights she wasn't out and about on some dashing escort's arm—openings, galas, red-carpet events. If it was on and it was *big*, thanks to Reggie and Grady Hamm, she was there.

Not that she spent the night with any of her escorts. Her intentions were always open but as the night progressed she'd spend more and more time comparing them to Blake and it didn't seem to matter that they'd just been named in the top one hundred beautiful people or had landed a lead role in a Hollywood blockbuster.

None of them measured up.

She knew Blake was just an anomaly and had he been around he'd tell her she was just obsessing about him purely because she couldn't have him.

But that didn't make him, or the lack of him, any less distracting.

And then Remembrance Sunday dawned, another fittingly bleak day, and Ava lay in bed with the covers pulled up to her chin, not even bothering to get up. She wondered if Blake was attending a service somewhere. Maybe hanging out in a pub with some of his army mates?

Maybe getting quietly drunk on his boat?

It was only a knock at her door around ten a.m. that roused her from her lethargy. For a moment she even contemplated not answering it, but hauled herself out of bed, throwing on a polar fleece gown, welcoming any distraction.

Or at least she'd thought so until she opened her door to find her mother, conspicuous by her absence these last couple of months, flirting with the press with all her brash blonde falseness. She'd been on Ibiza when Ava's house had been shot up and, apart from that one phone call, this was the first Ava had seen or heard of her for six months.

Sheila Kelly air-kissed Ava's face for the sake of the cameras and swept inside requesting a tour of the renovations. Ava shut the door on the 'give your mum a kiss, Ava' calls coming from the little clutch of paps and girded her loins.

She complied to her mother's request but was mentally preparing herself for the catch. For the ulterior motive.

Sheila cooed appreciatively at all the big-ticket items—at the roof and the pool and the acres of glass and steel—but sniffed dismissively at the homey wooden kitchen.

'You could pay a personal chef on what you earn,' she tutted.

And there it was, the entrée her mother was clearly looking for. Ava waited patiently for her mother to come out with it. 'Paul rang offering me another book deal,' she announced casually.

Ava barely supressed a snort at the mention of her ex-agent's name, now doing shonky off-shore deals in the literary field. She didn't understand how her mother could still associate with him. Ava reached for her handbag that was on the kitchen bench. 'How much this time?' she asked, pulling out her cheque book.

'A quarter of a million,' Sheila said. 'Since your little… scandal with Isobella, the price for a tell-all memoir has gone up considerably.'

Ava gritted her teeth. She paid her mother a generous allowance every month that kept her in houses and holidays, but she stopped by at least a couple of times a year for a top-up.

'I should just write it, darling,' Sheila said. 'Paul said it could be very lucrative for me. I wouldn't need to depend on you then.'

Ava snorted—she bet he had. 'No,' she said, signing the cheque. 'No tell-all. You write a single word and I will cut you off.' She tore it out of the book as noisily as she could.

Ava didn't care what her mother wrote about her—her twisted version of the truth. Ava knew the real story. But she didn't trust her mother not to tell lies about her father and that she couldn't tolerate. She wouldn't let her father's memory be besmirched.

'There's no need for that,' her mother replied waspishly as she took the cheque.

Ava folded her arms. 'Good.'

They stared at each other for a moment, then Sheila said, 'I'll be off, then.'

Ava nodded. Of course. Her mother had got what she'd

come for. There was no hug or air kisses this time—no cameras inside the house.

She watched as Sheila headed to the door and let herself out, surprised to find her hands were shaking as she put the cheque book back in her bag. A sense of being alone in the world assailed Ava, which, given how many people she had around her, was absurd in the extreme.

But she cursed her mother anyway, stupid tears in her eyes.

And before she knew what she was doing she was tracking back to her bedroom, picking up her phone off the bedside table and scrolling through her contacts.

Blake answered on the second ring. 'Hello?'

Ava shut her eyes, feeling foolish for having even rung him now, but his voice sounded so good.

'Hello?'

'Blake...'

There was a very definite pause at the other end before he said, 'Ava,' in a voice so wary she could practically cut the trepidation with a knife.

The tears built more insistently behind her eyes and she was glad she had them closed.

'Are you okay?'

Ava shook her head. 'No. Can you come over?'

Blake knew it was a bad idea when he left his boat the second her husky request was out. He knew it was a bad idea as he pulled up in front of Ava's house and four different cameras took pictures of him and one of the paps said, 'Hey, aren't you that builder guy?' He knew it was a bad idea when she answered the door in nothing but her dressing gown and a haughty look.

But it didn't stop him stepping inside when she pulled the door open. And it didn't stop him wanting to kiss her. It sure as hell didn't stop him *actually* kissing her when she shut the door, the haughtiness evaporating as she reached for him, and put her mouth to his.

Later he would come to know it as the FFK—the first fatal kiss—but in that moment nothing mattered. Not the two months of separation, not endless footage of her with other guys, not the giant divide in their lives so aptly demonstrated by the cameras on the other side of the door.

He just sucked her in, his senses filling with the smell and the taste of her as he pushed her hard against the nearby wall and devoured her mouth as if it were his last meal.

He groaned as she opened to him, kissed him back with equal vigour. He'd missed her—the feel and the smell and the taste of her. He'd missed her snooty little smile and the way she ate her food and her sexy, frilly lingerie hanging everywhere.

He missed her complete lack of inhibitions.

He missed the way she kissed—wide open and full throttle. The way he didn't have to duck and she didn't have to rise up on tippy-toe to align their mouths. The way her mouth was always just right there level with his and, God help him, always one hundred per cent willing.

Ava clung to Blake as the kiss went on and on. She hadn't realised how much she'd been starving for his mouth until it was on hers again.

And now it was time to feast.

'God, I missed you,' she said, pulling back slightly, their gazes meshing as she tried to catch her heavy breath, each oxygen molecule drowned in lashings of Blake.

Which was true—but not the full truth. She'd *more* than missed him. *She loved him.* As soon as she'd opened the door to him—no, before that—as soon as he'd knocked, she'd known.

Because he'd come.

She'd asked and he'd dropped everything to be here. No questions. Just action.

There'd only been two men in her life who'd done that

for her and she loved both of them too. One was her father. The other was Reggie.

And now there was Blake. Her big, brave, wounded warrior who had come without hesitation when she'd called. Who was looking at her with desire and lust but also with a healthy dose of wariness, his barriers fully up, clearly *not* loving her back.

So there was no way she could tell him—she'd learned a long time ago not to give *any* man that kind of power over you.

But she *could* show him.

She *could* love him with her body. And whisper it in her mind.

Blake sucked in a breath as the noise of his zip coming down sounded loud enough to be heard outside. He bit back a groan as her hand brushed his erection, reaching down to stop her, shutting his eyes as he dragged himself back from the lure of what could be.

His head spun with the effort and the sweet intoxication of her. He hadn't come for this.

No matter how much he wanted it.

Nothing had changed between them. If anything it had reverted to what it had always been. Ava crooking her finger and expecting him to come running.

Which he had.

He'd told her once he wasn't going to be her plaything and he meant it.

He captured her hand and pulled it up, trapping it against his chest as he leaned his forehead on hers and drew in some unsteady breaths. They both did.

When he felt under control again he eased back a little and said, 'What's this about, Ava?'

Ava felt all the desperation leach out of her at his calm enquiry. She let her head flop back against the wall. 'Sorry,' she said, her voice annoyingly husky. 'My mother was here. She always makes me a little crazy.'

'What did she want?'

Ava's gaze met his. 'The same thing she always wants. *Money*. Paul, who's now in publishing, keeps waving a tell-all book deal under her nose and I keep matching his offers.'

Blake's jaw clenched against a wave of disgust. What pieces of work they both were. 'Did you give it to her?'

Ava shrugged, hugging herself against how tawdry it all sounded. 'I've got the money.'

Blake shook his head at her wretchedness, his need to smash things duelling with her need to be comforted. He'd tried to forget in their two months apart how truly alone she was in the world but here it was in full Technicolor.

Sure, she might not have been short for an escort to a film premiere but she had no real family to look out for her.

Except Reggie.

And now him.

He took two calming breaths, then closed the short distance between them, his hands sliding to her hips. He could be outraged later. For now she really did need him.

He stroked a hand down her face. 'I'm sorry,' he said. 'What can I do?'

Ava gave him a half-smile as she slid her hand onto his arm. 'Right now? You can help me forget about my mother.'

Blake dropped his gaze to her mouth then flicked it up again, his resistance completely shot. 'Just once.'

Ava's smile broadened. 'Absolutely. But she's a *very* hard woman to forget. Might take you all day.'

Blake grinned.

CHAPTER THIRTEEN

TWO WEEKS LATER Blake was up late working on a kitchen design for a client when he heard dainty footsteps on the bow and then a familiar little knock and his pulse kicked up in anticipation.

They shouldn't still be doing this.

But they were.

He was *still* helping Ava forget her mother—every single night. All night long. They didn't seem to be able to stop no matter how much they said they were going to as she left each morning.

It was that first fatal kiss that had done it.

He'd been fine resisting the *notion* of her for two months—finishing his holiday, going back to work, getting on with his life. Fine with her image seemingly everywhere. Fine with opening the paper and reading about her. Fine to be the *friend* Ava had referred to in her media statement on her return to London, which hadn't lessened the speculation as to how she'd managed to lay so low for a week.

But then she'd kissed him and a wellspring of craving had erupted inside him and he *could not get enough*.

He certainly couldn't stop.

He'd broken the seal on his resistance and there was no way he was getting that sucker back. It had flown the coop and there was no hope of recapturing it.

But the worst thing was, it was more than sexual—how much more he didn't want to think about. He just knew he actually looked forward to her company—something he'd have never thought possible a few months ago.

It was as if there were two different Avas—the public persona, *Keep-out Kelly*, who left them wanting more with her *touch-me-not* smile and her ball-breaking business sense. And then there was the private persona. The one who let her guard down. The one who tramped onto his boat every night fresh from some red-carpet event schmoozing with the A-list eager to be with *him*. The one who cooked gourmet snacks for him in her underwear, who burped after she skulled half a can of beer, who smiled at him with her *touch-me-everywhere* smile.

Who left the boat every morning looking a hot mess and didn't seem to care.

Maybe that was part of the allure, the continuing of what they'd had for that week out on the canals. Where she could be nobody and they could be lovers and no one was around to care. No paps taking her picture or fans asking for her autograph.

Just him and her and their bubble.

The knock came again just as he'd almost reached the door and a muffled, 'Open up, I want to do unspeakable things to your body,' had him quickening the pace.

'I beg your pardon.' He grinned as he pushed open the door to a freezing London night to find her standing huddled into a long black coat buckled at the waist and her collar up to keep her neck warm. 'I object to being so outrageously objectified.'

'Oh, really?' Ava said, raising an eyebrow, unbuckling her coat and opening the lapels to reveal her nudity.

Blake's eyes widened as he forgot all about the bracing cold pushing icy fingers inside the boat, his gaze fixed on the hard points of her nipples.

'*Now* can I do unspeakable things to you?' she demanded.

Blake grabbed her hand. 'I am all yours,' he said as he pulled her inside.

Half an hour later they were lying in the dark together. Blake was drifting his fingers up and down her arm enhancing Ava's post-coital drowse. The urge to blurt out her feelings was never far away but something always held her back. She thought Blake might feel the same way, or at least feel something more than sex, but things were so perfect—she didn't want to rock the boat.

Literally or figuratively.

'I love this boat,' she said instead, rolling onto her side and snuggling into him. 'It's like my secret hideaway.'

Blake smiled. *'Mi casa es su casa,'* he said and surprised himself by how much he meant it. She *was* welcome here any time.

'It was my hideaway for a long time. It was like a…lifeline or something…somewhere to lick my wounds.'

Ava brushed her lips against his shoulder. If anyone had needed a place to lick his wounds it had been Blake. If she'd gone through what he'd endured, she'd still be holed up in a drunken stupor.

'You mentioned once that you'd received some news that made you realise there were worse things than having one leg. Do you mind me asking what it was?'

Blake stared at the ceiling for long moments.

'One of the guys in my unit…he had the same thing happen to him about six months after me, lost a leg. But…'

Blake hesitated. He'd never told anyone about this. But it felt right unburdening himself to Ava, especially in their private little bubble.

'He also had his genitals blown off.'

Ava gasped, rising up on her elbow to look down at him. 'That's…terrible.'

She felt absurd tears prick the backs of her eyes as she tried to grapple with what that must mean to a person. How would she like to go through her life never being able to be physically intimate?

Blake saw the shine in her eyes as he reached out to tuck a stray strand of caramel hair that had fallen forward behind Ava's ear and he gave her a gentle smile.

His Ava was surprisingly mushy on the inside.

His Ava. The thought was equal parts terrifying and tantalising.

'It made me rethink my attitude, that's for sure. I mean, there I was, essentially fully functional, while some guys… they're never going to be fully functional. At least I could still have sex. Still…' he looked into Ava's yellow-green eyes shining with compassion '…make love to a woman.'

Ava's heart felt like a boulder in her chest. She shifted, moved over him until she was lying on top of him, her forehead pressed into his neck, his heartbeat loud in her ear. His arms wrapped around her body and a tear slid out of her eye.

After a few moments she raised her head to look down at him. 'Make love to me,' she whispered.

Blake lifted his head and kissed her. He should say no. They weren't supposed to be dragging this impossible thing out. But he couldn't. He wanted to do exactly as she'd asked.

So he rolled her over and made love like there was no tomorrow.

Ava felt a lot more sombre the next morning as he saw her off the boat. The plight of the soldier he'd told her about last night had wormed its way under her skin and she held him a little longer, kissed him a little deeper. Usually Blake stayed inside the warmth of the boat as she exited but it was as if he could sense her sadness, and even though he was only in his boxer briefs and T-shirt he climbed out with her and held her for as long as she needed.

'You okay?' he asked as she finally pulled away.

She very nearly confessed then and there, but she felt absurdly close to tears again and she doubted she could get it out without being a big snotty mess and she had a magazine shoot to get to in just over an hour.

She gave him a small smile and a nod. And even though she knew she shouldn't ask she said, 'See you tonight?'

He kissed her. And even though he knew he shouldn't agree, that they should be ending this, he said, 'Tonight.'

But by two o'clock in the afternoon everything had changed.

Blake was at work when he got the first inkling of the storm that was about to take over his life. He was at his desk when he looked up to see Joanna and Charlie approaching and his keen sense of doom kicked into overdrive.

They pulled up in front of his desk looking like they did that day a few years ago they'd called by the boat together—a united front—ready for an intervention. 'What?' he asked warily.

Joanna fiddled with his stapler. 'I've just seen you on the telly.'

Blake frowned. *'What?'*

'On the news. Pictures of you,' she clarified. 'And Ava. On the boat.'

Blake's frown deepened. 'During my holiday?' he asked.

'Umm…no,' Joanna said, putting his stapler down and picking up a ruler, tapping it lightly on his desk. 'Apparently they were…taken this morning.'

Charlie folded his arms across his chest and eyeballed his brother. 'You *are* shagging her.'

Joanna dug Charlie hard in the ribs and he grabbed his side.

Blake stood as his mind went back to this morning. To kissing her goodbye out in the open. Not that he'd been looking, but he certainly hadn't noticed a clutch of paps. Maybe someone on a neighbouring boat recognised her and decided to make a quid or two?

'What kind of pictures?' he asked.

'I'm-shagging-Ava-Kelly pictures,' Charlie said. 'Or at least that's what your hand on her arse and your tongue down her throat says to me.'

'I mean do they look clear? Are they professional or amateur?'

'You can tell it's you and her *very* clearly,' Charlie said. 'But it looks like they were taken from a distance, like you see in all those magazines, with a telephoto lens or something.'

Blake plopped back onto his chair. Photographers had been staking out his boat? Had they followed her or had someone tipped them off?

The very thought gave him the creeps.

'What did they say about the pictures?' he asked.

'They were wondering who you are and if you were Ava's latest,' Joanna said, still tapping the ruler. 'If you were the friend she'd hidden away with for that week she'd dropped out...stuff like that.'

Blake didn't know how to feel about the news except for the fact that it probably made it easier to make the break they should have made a fortnight ago.

Which should have made him relieved.

It didn't.

'Oh, well, I guess it pays to be nobody, huh?' he dismissed absently.

Joanne and Charlie looked at each other and Blake's skin prickled with unease. The tapping of the ruler got louder and Blake snatched it out of Joanna's hand. 'Just say it,' he said.

'They're already speculating about...your leg,' she said.

Blake frowned. *His leg?* Of course...his boxers this morning would have been no match for a telephoto lens.

'Must be a slow news day. I'm sure everyone will move on soon.'

He sure hoped so because the idea of a lens trained on his boat was a little too reminiscent of a rifle sight for his liking.

Joanna shook her head. 'The pictures are practically going viral online and on social media,' she said, her voice doubtful. 'The British press are still all dying to know where Ava went for that week... The whole thing with Grady Hamm has caused a huge stir, Blake. Combine that with the pretty intense interest her love life has always roused and I don't know that this is going to blow over so soon.'

Blake's phone rang. 'It's Ava,' he said as he answered the call.

'There's photos of us on the news.'

Blake almost laughed at her panicked opener. No pre-amble—just straight to the point. 'Yes. I know.'

'I'm *so, so* sorry. They must have followed me.'

Blake shrugged. 'Yeh, but I'm not anybody so...I'm sure it'll all blow over.'

Her groan was Blake's first indication that he might be underestimating the situation. 'Blake...they're going to know who you are within hours. Their editors are going to want to know every single thing about you and I wouldn't be surprised if it's in all the evening papers. There's prob-ably someone going through your rubbish right now.'

Blake laughed. 'Why would they want to go through *my* rubbish?'

'*Because your hand is on my arse,*' she said testily. 'And they don't know who you are, which is driving them crazy. It's only going to be a matter of time before one of them re-alises you're the guy who was at my place for three months.'

Blake couldn't believe they'd be interested in a guy like him. 'And when they do they'll find there's nothing very exciting about me at all and they'll move on.'

'Oh, Blake. You don't know how intrusive this is… How could you?'

Her tone was hopeless and he started to worry. For her. 'I'm a big boy, Ava. I'm sure I'll cope.'

'I don't think you should go to the boat tonight.'

'What?'

'I think they'll be waiting for you. They're kind of persistent.'

And then it really dawned on him what she was saying. 'So…you're not coming tonight?'

'No.'

Blake tried to rein in his disappointment. A part of him could see it was a good thing—something they should have done a fortnight ago—but part of him didn't want to let go either.

'You know if you didn't want to come…if you wanted it over, you could just say.'

'Blake…no.' Her voice was instantly dismissive and he believed her. 'Trust me, you're not going to want me where they'll be. Maybe we can meet somewhere else. A hotel, maybe?'

'A hotel?' Blake couldn't believe what she was saying. 'You want a place that charges by the hour or do you prefer your *usual* suite?'

'Blake…please…I'm just trying to save you from this. It's probably going to get ugly.'

Blake snorted. *As if he cared about ugly.* It sounded like she was more interested in saving herself and her rep to him.

Fine by him.

He should never have let it get this far anyway. 'Well, you do what you've got to do,' he said tersely and hung up.

He looked at Joanna and Charlie, who had clearly been listening. 'What are *you* going to do?' Joanna asked.

Blake rolled his eyes. 'I'm going to finish up here for the day, then I'm going to go home.'

Charlie and Joanna exchanged looks and Blake resolutely ignored them.

* * *

By nightfall, Blake had changed his tune. The evening papers were full of his arse grope and when he was heading down the walkway to his boat's permanent mooring it was surrounded by paps. A few months back he wouldn't have known a paparazzo if he'd fallen over one—now he was all too familiar with them.

He'd backed away and ended up at Charlie's place with Joanna flicking between news stations.

Ava rang and texted several times but Blake, feeling grimmer and grimmer as the night progressed, did not feel like talking. By the time he'd bunked down on the couch the press knew his name, rank and serial number. By the time he woke in the morning they knew a lot more than that.

Charlie had got up early to buy all the tabloids and it was clear no part of Blake's life had been considered sacred.

Ava had been right—he'd had *no* idea how voracious the press could be. His army record was there for anyone, anywhere to read. His tours, the units he'd served with, the explosion and his subsequent amputation with a close-up of his prosthesis.

One paper exploited his military record with the head-line—*Ava's Crippled War Hero.* Another took a different tack with—*The Carpenter and the Lady.* They'd got comments from his neighbours, people he used to serve with and clients he'd worked with.

But the hardest thing of all was the big splash about his commendation. His *act of heroism* was recounted in all its trumped-up glory. Blake felt ill. The news was making him out to be some kind of Second Coming and all he could see was Pete dying in the back of a military ambulance. Colin, lying dead in the dirt while he cried out in pain.

So many men dead and permanently maimed and this... *crap* was all they cared about?

How would the men he'd served with, *men who were*

still serving, still putting themselves on the line, feel about all this?

He was so angry he wanted to smash things with his bare hands. Angry about frivolous 'news' and first-world privilege, but mostly about confirming something he'd always known deep down—he couldn't live like this. Under constant scrutiny.

Ava and he were worlds apart and they never should have crossed the divide.

This was his worst-case scenario and he was living it.

His life was under the magnifying glass along with the lives of everyone he'd ever touched. People who'd never asked for this.

These last two weeks had been some of the happiest of his life. But this...nightmare was the flipside.

'Blake?' Joanna squeezed his shoulder and handed him a coffee. He took it and scooted over so she could sit beside him. 'They're not lying, Blake. I know you find this hard to take, but what you did *does* make you a hero to a lot of people.'

'Do you think Colin would say that?' he demanded and hated that he'd made her flinch.

Joanna recovered quickly and looked him straight in the eye. 'Colin would say it most of all.' She squeezed his knee. 'You were always his hero. He looked up to you. He was proud to serve with you. But you know what, Blake? He would have done it anyway. With or without you. What happened to him could have happened at *any* time.'

Blake shut his eyes against the way out in words. It could have-but it didn't. It happened on *his* watch.

A knock interrupted them. 'That'll be Ava,' Joanna announced, pushing herself up.

Blake almost choked on his first sip of coffee. 'And how *does* Ava know I'm here?'

'I told her, *stooped.*' Joanna grinned. 'She's my new best friend, didn't you know? Besties tell each other everything.'

'Joanna.' His voice held a warning.

'You have to talk to her, Blake. She's worried about you.'

'It's not going to work out between us, Joanna, so you can just stop planning the hen night.'

Joanna shook her head. 'Well, then, you're an idiot. She's the best thing that ever happened to you, Blake.'

CHAPTER FOURTEEN

BLAKE OPENED HIS mouth to rebuff Joanna but she was already heading towards the door and before he knew it Ava was standing in front of him and he was standing too.

She was wearing what appeared to be a very expensive, very glittery tracksuit, her hair up in a ponytail.

And she looked as if she hadn't slept a wink either.

She took a step towards him but his, 'I hope no paps followed you because I do not want Charlie and Trudy embroiled in this circus,' stopped her in her tracks.

Ava sucked in a breath against the hostility in his tone. It was as if the last five and a half months hadn't happened at all and they were back at square one.

'I know a thing or two about shaking the press,' she said tersely.

Blake snorted. 'Apparently not enough.'

'Look, I'm sorry,' she sighed. 'I never wanted this to happen.'

'And yet here we are.'

Ava shoved her hands into her pockets. Her fingers were freezing and it didn't have much to do with the cold November morning. 'Reggie's working on it,' she said. 'We can fix it. We can salvage it. I'm going to put out a statement.'

'Saying what?' he demanded.

Ava took a deep breath. Time to lay her cards on the table. She hadn't wanted it to be like this but fate had forced her hand. 'Well, we could deny it. Say that we're just friends. Or…we could say that our relationship is new and we'd like privacy while we explore it.'

Blake blinked. *What the*? 'So I can be your bit of rough?' he snapped. 'The *carpenter* to your *lady*? Or some…pity-screw to make the *crippled* war hero feel better about himself?'

Ava shut her eyes against the ugliness of the headlines he'd just thrown in her face and the contempt in his voice. He had every right to be angry. Tears built behind her lids but she forced them back. His life had been turned upside down because of her—it wasn't the time for stupid girly tears.

'I'm sorry about what they're saying,' she said, opening her eyes. 'About what they've revealed. If I could turn back the clock, believe me, Blake, I would. But I'm *not* sorry you're being recognised for what you did. You deserve those accolades.'

Blake shook his head. She didn't get it. She really didn't get it. The men who'd died, who were still fighting—they were the ones who deserved the accolades.

'Pete *died*, Ava. I don't want his family reading all about the *hero* who didn't *quite* manage to save their loved one in the newspapers, dragging up all their grief again. Thinking I'm using his death as some cheap publicity stunt to pull a supermodel.'

Ava felt the cold from outside seep inside her at his suggestion. *Surely no one would think that?*

'Don't you think it's hard *enough* for them this time of year, with Christmas around the corner?'

Ava felt helpless. She was used to this level of intrusion from the press, immune to it in a lot of ways, but she still remembered how shocking it had been in the beginning.

'I'm sorry for them that it's being dragged up,' she murmured. 'But I for one think heroism should be celebrated. Too often we celebrate beauty and money and power and yet there are guys like you, defending the free world. I think we should recognise heroes more often.'

Blake ran a hand through his hair. 'You don't get it,' he said bitterly. 'I don't want to be a hero, Ava. Men are still over there. Others are *dead.*'

Sometimes, when he woke in the middle of night, the guilt over that was more than he could bear. He looked over her shoulder and caught Joanna's eye before returning his gaze to Ava.

'I'm *not* going to cash in on *their* accolades.'

Ava felt almost paralysed by the hard line of rejection running through his voice. He hadn't even been this harsh with her in the beginning and her pulse hammered a frantic beat against her wrist.

She didn't want to lose him. She couldn't.

'Fine. What about just being my hero, then?'

Ava moved in closer until there was just a coffee table separating them. She knew if she didn't say it now she never would. And maybe if she'd said it earlier they wouldn't be where they were. 'I love you.'

It took Blake a few seconds to compute the revelation. And even then it was too hard to wrap his head around. *'What?'* he spluttered. *Love?* That was the most ridiculous thing he'd ever heard. 'I thought this was just…a fling, a… casual thing.'

Ava put her hand on her hip, her fingers digging in hard at his rejection, at his trivialisation of her love. She'd never told any man she loved him before and it felt like a knife to the heart to be so summarily dismissed.

'Really? Is that what you thought?' she asked scathingly.

This was a lot more than a casual fling between them and they both knew it.

'Really?' she repeated. 'All those things we've been through, all those nights lying in bed talking and talking and talking? That was just casual?'

Blake didn't even try to pretend she wasn't right. Ava

had been a bright spot in what had become a pretty beige life. A life he'd thought was fine. But never would be again.

He folded his arms as he cut right to the crux. 'I can't live in a goldfish bowl.'

Ava bit her lip. His words sounded so final and she swore she could hear her heart breaking over the silence in the room. 'I'm not *just* a girl on a boat, Blake. I *never* was. That goldfish bowl is my life for the conceivable future.'

Blake nodded. 'I know. But I don't want any part of it.'

She put her hand on one folded forearm feeling suddenly desperate, tears threatening again. 'So that's it?' she asked, her voice wobbling. 'You're not even going to fight for us? You can fight for this country but not for me?'

Blake hardened himself to the injury in her voice. Only Ava could be so dramatic. 'There isn't an us,' he said testily.

'Please,' Ava whispered, her hand tightening around his arm. There *was* something between them. She knew it. And she knew it could be good. 'We could make it work. We just have to want it bad enough.'

Her plea cut right to his heart but Blake shut it down. He'd had enough of complicated in his life. He'd sensed right from the beginning that she was going to be trouble and he'd been right.

Now his face was splashed all over the national newspapers. *Pete's* life and death splashed about too. Blake's grief and his guilt staring back at him in black and white for the entire nation to share.

All he'd wanted when he'd got things back on track was to have a quiet conflict-free life.

A life with Ava would be *neither* of those things.

Blake dropped his arms and her hand fell away. 'I don't want it bad enough,' he said and turned away.

And this time Ava did hear the crack as her heart split wide open.

The following wintery weeks were the perfect foil for Ava's mood. Christmas in London was always beautiful as decorative lights went up everywhere and the Christmas tree arrived in Trafalgar Square, but Ava didn't really notice. She didn't notice the roasting chestnuts vendors or the ice skaters at Hyde Park or the elaborately dressed windows in the department stores.

It was all too bright and sparkly for her when inside she identified more with the barren trees than the gay lights of Oxford Street.

She was merely going through the motions. Smiling and talking when she needed to and just trying to get through the rest. The media, as always, nipped at her heels but it was pleasing to note they'd stopped camping out regularly at Blake's boat since she'd denied their relationship in a press release, citing him as a friend only.

It didn't mean she stopped thinking about him. Stopped wishing in her darkest hours that she *were* that girl on the boat. It just made it easier to bear not to have to see his face next to hers on the news or in the papers every day.

But Christmas Eve came around quicker than she'd hoped and she knew she was going to have to face him again. The charity gala was the event of the year and, as the new patron, Ava was expected not only to attend but to shine.

And that was exactly what she told herself as she dressed to the nines. She had a certain image to project—glamour and sophistication—and she had every intention of wowing Joanna and all the others who had paid five thousand quid a head to ride the London Eye with her for a couple of hours.

Including Blake.

She wore a plush crimson, long-sleeved velvet gown that clung to her body and swept to the floor in a short train. A fur-trimmed hoodie attached to the back set it off and loaned her a touch of the regal when she smiled for the cameras with her famous haughty smile in front of an illuminated Eye.

And she spent the next three hours in a glass bubble, sipping champagne, laughing and chatting with people, new ones with each revolution. Smiling until her face ached, forcing herself not to search the bubbles above and around her for the one person she wanted to see the most.

Maybe he hadn't come?

On her second-last revolution for the night, Joanna and her founding partners along with some of the charity workers joined her and Ava relaxed a little. They talked about the success of the night and the upcoming events for the New Year and where she could help out. They also talked about their husbands, about how much they'd loved Christmas and Ava listened as they laughed and smiled at fond memories.

About five minutes from the revolution ending Joanna manoeuvred Ava to one side. She smiled at her and said, 'You know Blake's here, right.'

Ava nodded. 'I assumed he was.'

'You should talk with him.'

Ava gave a sad smile. 'I don't think your brother wants to talk to me.'

Joanna narrowed her eyes. 'You love him, right?'

Ava blinked and then laughed. Joanna was definitely a Walker—no subtlety. 'Yes.'

'So talk to him.'

Ava shook her head. 'He was pretty angry.'

Joanna regarded her for a moment or two and Ava felt as if she was being weighed up. 'Do you know the soldier that was killed the day Blake was injured was my husband?'

Ava's nodded. 'Yes. He told me when we were on the boat.'

Joanna looked taken aback. 'The last thing I said to Blake when they left for their tour was to look after Colin for me, to bring him home safe.' Joanna paused. 'He's not angry at you. He's angry at himself. That he's alive when so many aren't. That he *survived*. Every time he has fun or lets himself go, the guilt bites him hard.'

Ava's heart broke all over again for Blake. He shouldn't have to live his life eclipsed by guilt because he made it through when others didn't. 'I...didn't know that. I mean, I know he feels guilt about Colin...about the commendation...but not about surviving.'

Joanna grimaced. 'Well, he's not much of a talker. But I do know he was happy when he was with you and that he's never told *anyone* about Colin except for his shrink. I don't know if he'll ever be able to fully let go of the guilt and that's his *real* wound, not his leg. But I think if anyone can help him heal it's you.'

Ava couldn't agree more. But...'I can't if he won't let me in.'

The capsules were coming back down to the exit platform again and everyone was gathering at the door to clear the capsule in time for it moving on to the next platform where it would load again for the last revolution of the night.

'Well, they do say absence makes the heart grow fonder, right? And anyway, it's Christmas, it's the time for miracles.'

Joanna smiled and pointed to her brother standing rather grimly amongst the dozen people patiently waiting to get on.

Ava's gaze devoured him in all his tuxedoed glory. Who'd have thought a man who looked so good in a tool belt and a T-shirt could look just as good in a tux?

'Good luck,' Joanna whispered as she joined the exodus.

Ava sighed as Blake's gaze meshed with hers and he gave her a grim nod of his head.

She was going to need more than a miracle.

Blake had barely been able to take his eyes off her all night. Whatever capsule he'd been in, he'd tracked her movements, his sight starved of her for weeks now. And the second he entered the capsule and was offered a glass of champagne he took two and made a beeline for her.

He'd planned to patiently wait his turn and then make polite conversation with her, but as soon as the door had shut behind him the aura surrounding her grabbed him by the gut and yanked hard as a tumult of emotion flooded his chest.

What a fool he'd been.

He loved her.

And he didn't care how much anyone had paid for some time in her company, he was monopolising all of it.

'I've been an idiot,' he said as he elbowed someone else aside and handed her the glass of champagne.

Ava blinked as Blake's broad magnificence filled her vision. 'You…have?'

He nodded. It might have come totally out of the blue for Blake but he knew it as surely as he'd known he'd wanted to serve his country.

'Yes. I don't talk a lot and I'm not into staring at my navel and blabbing about my feelings. But I do believe in the truth and I've been lying to myself these past few weeks. Only I didn't realise it until right now. I thought I was doing so well and then I see you tonight and I realise that I'm in love with you and these last few weeks have been…*crap.*'

Ava looked around, pretty sure *everyone* was eavesdropping. 'You…love me?'

He nodded, wondering if she was going to stay monosyllabic for the rest of the night. 'Yes.'

'Oh.' Ava's heart tripped in her chest. *Well, that she hadn't expected.* Neither, she suspected, had Joanna.

It looked as if it was her night for miracles after all.

The temptation to let herself go and fling herself into his arms was enormous but there were still a lot of obstacles in their path and she needed to be sure. She needed *him* to be sure. 'What about the goldfish bowl?'

Blake sighed. 'I still can't live like that, Ava. But I was wrong a few weeks ago—*I do want it bad enough*. So I guess we're going to have to figure that one out. Compromise a little. Because I *want* this. I want you.'

Ava smiled at him for the first time, relief flushing through her veins making her almost dizzy. She reached out a hand and grasped his lapel, steadying herself. 'Well, I guess we could find somewhere to live that's more secure and not so accessible to the media?'

Blake slid his hand onto hers and held it against his chest. 'And you could stop feeding them gourmet snacks,' he suggested with affectionate exasperation, slipping his other hand onto her hip. 'And getting Reggie to report your movements to them so they know where you are every moment of every day.'

Ava nodded. 'I could do that. I could also set limits with them over you and your information. I've not done it before but I know others do and…I think you're a pretty good trade-off.' She grinned.

Blake pulled her in closer. 'And I promise to *try* not to punch every man who touches you during a photo shoot or a commercial or whatever you're doing for work.'

Ava felt stupidly teary at this concession. She knew how hard that would be for his Neanderthal, Bionic-Man streak. 'Thank you,' she whispered.

Blake smiled at her, wanting desperately to kiss her, to push her up against the glass and show her how much he loved her, but knowing they needed to talk first. 'And clearly, you can't live on a boat so I could sell it.'

'No way,' Ava objected. 'Keep that. I have very…' she ran her fingers under his lapel, feeling the firmness of his chest beneath the superb cut '…fond memories there,' she said, her smile widening.

He leaned in and nuzzled her neck. 'You're right. We'll keep the boat.'

Ava's heart dared to sing as she sank in closer to him.

'But is it going to be enough for you?' she asked, pulling back slightly.

Blake looked down into her yellow-green eyes. The whole Thames was stretched out behind her, the Houses of Parliament and Big Ben illuminated in a soft orange glow, a truly magnificent sight. But he only had eyes for Ava.

For the woman he loved.

'It's a start. And we'll get better at it. We have to, because I'm miserable without you.'

'Me too,' Ava admitted. But still her mind wandered to her conversation with Joanna and Ava felt anxious all over again. 'Joanna told me you feel guilty about surviving the war when Colin, when others, didn't,' she said.

Blake felt the usual punch to his gut at the mention of Colin's name. 'Did she now?'

Ava looked into his eyes because she needed to be sure that he understood what she was saying. 'I don't pretend to know what you went through, Blake. And I don't pretend to think it can be fixed through love alone. I know you're not a talker but I don't want you to shut me out either. I want to know *all* of you. Even the bits you don't want me to know. I can't be part of a relationship where you hide away all the dark bits…all the sad bits. I can't promise to know how to handle them, but I *do* want to try. I need you to promise that you'll *talk* to me. That *nothing* will be off-limits.'

Blake took a moment or two to absorb what she was asking. Opening up had never been easy for him, but he'd never met someone who'd meant so much to him either. He knew this woman in his arms and she was warm and sexy and giving and nothing like the woman he'd first thought her to be. She'd taken the risk and opened up to him, put her trust in him, surely he could do the same?

Because she was definitely worth fighting for.

'I promise,' he said. 'I don't promise I'll be very articulate but I promise to talk to you.'

Ava's heart swelled in her chest. She knew that couldn't have been easy for him. 'That's all I want.'

And for long moments they just looked at each other, absorbing all the details of each other's faces, trying to imprint this memory on their retinas for ever.

'You know there's going to be a bit of a frenzy to start with, don't you?' Ava warned.

'That's fine,' Blake said, lifting his hand to push the hoodie back off her hair. 'Let's just not feed it, huh?'

Ava nodded. 'Deal.'

Blake smiled down into her face. 'You're so beautiful,' he said. 'I can't believe it took me all this time to figure out I loved you.'

'I can,' Ava murmured. 'It took you a million pounds to even pay me any attention.'

Blake chuckled. 'I love you,' he said.

Ava sighed at the healing power of three little words as her heart felt whole again. And she was going to spend the rest of her life with her wounded warrior, helping him to feel whole again also. 'I love you too,' she said.

Their lips met and Ava felt as if it were New Year's Eve instead of Christmas Eve as fireworks popped and sparkled behind her eyes.

The sound of a dozen mingled sighs and the burst of spontaneous applause in the capsule added to the celebration as did the pop and flare of paparazzi lenses far below.

Best. Christmas. Ever.

* * * * *

Mills & Boon® Hardback
December 2013

ROMANCE

Defiant in the Desert	Sharon Kendrick
Not Just the Boss's Plaything	Caitlin Crews
Rumours on the Red Carpet	Carole Mortimer
The Change in Di Navarra's Plan	Lynn Raye Harris
The Prince She Never Knew	Kate Hewitt
His Ultimate Prize	Maya Blake
More than a Convenient Marriage?	Dani Collins
A Hunger for the Forbidden	Maisey Yates
The Reunion Lie	Lucy King
The Most Expensive Night of Her Life	Amy Andrews
Second Chance with Her Soldier	Barbara Hannay
Snowed in with the Billionaire	Caroline Anderson
Christmas at the Castle	Marion Lennox
Snowflakes and Silver Linings	Cara Colter
Beware of the Boss	Leah Ashton
Too Much of a Good Thing?	Joss Wood
After the Christmas Party...	Janice Lynn
Date with a Surgeon Prince	Meredith Webber

MEDICAL

From Venice with Love	Alison Roberts
Christmas with Her Ex	Fiona McArthur
Her Mistletoe Wish	Lucy Clark
Once Upon a Christmas Night...	Annie Claydon

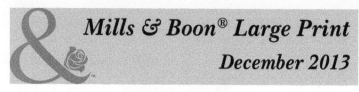

Mills & Boon® Large Print

December 2013

ROMANCE

The Billionaire's Trophy	Lynne Graham
Prince of Secrets	Lucy Monroe
A Royal Without Rules	Caitlin Crews
A Deal with Di Capua	Cathy Williams
Imprisoned by a Vow	Annie West
Duty at What Cost?	Michelle Conder
The Rings That Bind	Michelle Smart
A Marriage Made in Italy	Rebecca Winters
Miracle in Bellaroo Creek	Barbara Hannay
The Courage To Say Yes	Barbara Wallace
Last-Minute Bridesmaid	Nina Harrington

HISTORICAL

Not Just a Governess	Carole Mortimer
A Lady Dares	Bronwyn Scott
Bought for Revenge	Sarah Mallory
To Sin with a Viking	Michelle Willingham
The Black Sheep's Return	Elizabeth Beacon

MEDICAL

NYC Angels: Making the Surgeon Smile	Lynne Marshall
NYC Angels: An Explosive Reunion	Alison Roberts
The Secret in His Heart	Caroline Anderson
The ER's Newest Dad	Janice Lynn
One Night She Would Never Forget	Amy Andrews
When the Cameras Stop Rolling...	Connie Cox